The first day of school.

My friend Judéwin knew a few words of English and had overheard the woman talk about cutting our long hair. Our mothers had taught us that only warriors who were captured had their hair shingled by the enemy. Among our people short hair was worn by mourners, and shingled hair by cowards.

I resisted by kicking and scratching wildly. I was carried downstairs and tied fast in a chair.

I cried aloud, shaking my head until I felt the cold blades of the scissors and heard them gnaw off one of my thick braids. Then I lost my spirit. Since I had been taken from my mother, I had suffered extreme indignities. People had stared at me. I had been tossed in the air like a wooden puppet. And now my long hair was being shingled like a coward's. I moaned for my mother, but no one came to comfort me. For now I was only one of many little animals driven by a herder.

Zitkala-Ša. (Courtesy of the Historical Photograph Collections, Washington State University Libraries.)

The Flight of Red Bird

THE LIFE OF ZITKALA-ŠA

Re-created from the writings of
Zitkala-Ša
and the research of
Doreen Rappaport

PUFFIN BOOKS

PUFFIN BOOKS
Published by the Penguin Group
Penguin Putnam Books for Young Readers,
345 Hudson Street, New York, New York 10014, U.S.A.
Penguin Books Ltd, 27 Wrights Lane, London W8 5TZ, England
Penguin Books Australia Ltd, Ringwood, Victoria, Australia
Penguin Books Canada Ltd, 10 Alcorn Avenue, Toronto, Ontario, Canada M4V 3B2
Penguin Books (N.Z.) Ltd, 182-190 Wairau Road, Auckland 10, New Zealand

Penguin Books Ltd, Registered Offices: Harmondsworth, Middlesex, England

First published in the United States of America by Dial Books,
a division of Penguin Books USA Inc., 1997
Published by Puffin Books,
a member of Penguin Putnam Books for Young Readers, 1999

1 3 5 7 9 10 8 6 4 2

THE LIBRARY OF CONGRESS HAS CATALOGED THE DIAL EDITION AS FOLLOWS:
Rappaport, Doreen.
The flight of Red Bird: the life of Zitkala-Ša / re-created from the writings of Zitkala-Ša
and the research of Doreen Rappaport.
p. cm.
Includes bibliographical references and index.
Summary: Chronicles, through her own reminiscences, letters, speeches, and stories,
the experiences of a Yankton Indian woman whose life spanned the end of
the nineteenth and beginning of the twentieth century.
ISBN 0-8037-1438-6
1. Zitkala-Ša, 1876–1938. 2. Yankton women—Biography. 3. Yankton Indians—Civil
rights. 4. Yankton Indians—Government relations. 5. Indians, Treatment of—Great
Plains. 6. United States—Race relations. [1. Zitkala-Ša, 1876–1938. 2. Yankton
Indians—Biography. 3. Indians of North America—Great Plains—Biography.
4. Women—Biography.] I. Title.
E99.Y25Z55 1997 973'.04975'0092 [B]—DC20 96-18339 CIP AC

Puffin Books ISBN 0-14-130465-0

Printed in the United States of America

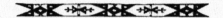

Native American motif by Ruth White Horse

For Tom D'Amico,
who taught me how to fly

CONTENTS

ACKNOWLEDGMENTS

Deborah Sue Welch's scholarship in her pioneering dissertation on Zitkala-Ša gave me the courage to begin this book; she read my manuscript and at every turn shared her knowledge and insight with me. The books on the history of the Yanktons by Shirley Bernie, Leonard Bruguier, and Renée Sansom-Flood made available information previously known only to members of the Yankton nation. Lyndall Callan; Elizabeth Diggs; P. Jane Hafen, Assistant Professor, University of Nevada, Las Vegas, NV; Emily Arnold McCully; Ruth Rosenberg; and William Willard, Director, Native American Studies, Washington State University, Pullman, WA, read drafts of the book and offered supportive, critical comments. Jessie Hafen brought her unique expertise to her reading. Arlene Hirschfelder and Eli Zaretsky, Associate Professor, University of Missouri, Columbia, MO, went beyond friendship and generosity in answering my numerous requests to have them reread the manuscript. Raymond J. DeMallie, Professor and Director of the American Indian Studies Research Institute, Indiana University, Bloomington, IN, and Agnes Picotte, Director, Ella C. Deloria Research Project, Chamberlain, SD, helped me with chapter names and to prepare the glossary. Jo Allyn Archambault, Director of the American Indian Program, National Museum of Natural History (Smithsonian) identified the origin of Zitkala-Ša's traditional dress. Drs. Richard Weininger, Gretchen Stearns, and William Lloyd helped me try to decipher Zitkala-Ša's medical difficulties.

The following persons graciously shepherded me through the laby-

◆ ◆ *Acknowledgments* ◆ ◆

rinths of special collections to pertinent correspondence, photographs, interviews, newspaper articles, and other background material: John Aubrey, Ayer Librarian, Ayer Collection, Newberry Library, Chicago, IL; Dr. Leonard Bruguier, Director, and Margaret Quintal, Assistant Director, Institute of American Indian Studies, University of South Dakota, Vermillion, SD; Doris Burton, Uintah County Historian and Regional History Center Librarian, Uintah County Library, Vernal, UT; Pat Etter, Department of Archives and Manuscripts, University Libraries, Arizona State University, Tempe, AZ; Mark Field, Marquette University, Milwaukee, WI; Joy and Richard Norton, who so meticulously indexed the *Vernal Express* that I accomplished in one day what would have taken me many weeks; Thomas D. Hamm, Archivist, Lilly Library, Earlham College, Richmond, IN; Jean La Reau, Oklahoma Historical Society, Oklahoma City, OK; Karen Zimmerman, Archivist, the I. D. Weeks Library, University of South Dakota, Vermillion, SD; Barbara Landis, Cumberland County Historical Society, Carlisle, PA; LaVera Rose, South Dakota State Archives, Pierre, SD; John Selch, Reference Librarian, Indiana State Library, Indianapolis, IN; Harry Thompson, Curator and Managing Editor, The Center for Western Studies, Augustana College, Sioux Falls, SD.

I am especially grateful to David Whittaker, Curator, Archives of the Mormon Experience, Harold B. Lee Library, Brigham Young University, Provo, UT, who dug the Raymond and Gertrude Bonnin Papers out of storage and put up with my many requests as he was trying to get ready for a sabbatical abroad. Others at Brigham Young University who helped were Scott Duvall, Chad Flake, Dennis Rowley, and Tom Wells. John and Ruth Ann Parker generously shared their research notes on White's Institute. As always, Bob Dumont, Jim Falconi, and

◆ ◆ *Acknowledgments* ◆ ◆

Phil Yockey of the research division of the New York Public Library answered my many requests for material from other libraries.

Gordon Shields, Administrative Officer of the Yankton nation, arranged for LaVonne Hare to take me around the Yankton Reservation. Violet M. Schildt and Nadine Auld took me around the Uintah and Ouray Reservations. Agnes, Norbert, and Mabel Picotte shared their lives and arranged for me to meet Hazel Ashes, Zitkala-Ša's niece. Richard Curry and Hazel Ashes shared personal details about their families; Hazel's wonderful humor, keen intelligence, and extensive knowledge of her people's language enriched my life far beyond the pages of this book. Stays at the Virginia Center for the Creative Arts and the Mary Anderson Center for the Arts provided the necessary solitude for work. Special thanks to Sarah Roberson Yates, Director of the Mary Anderson Center, and the fathers and brothers of Mt. St. Francis, for their generosity and good humor.

My friends in the Bank Street Writers' Workshop offered encouragement and supportive criticism throughout. "Copyeditor extraordinaire" Renée Vera Cafiero cleaned up my act. Again I am indebted to the creativity, professionalism, and teamwork of the people at Dial who cared as passionately as I did about the integrity of this book: Cindy Weissler kept this book on schedule when it seemed impossible to do so; Nancy R. Leo carefully studied the text so her book design would match the dignity of Zitkala-Ša's life; Michele A. Foley astounded me with her scholarship and her eye for detail that never loses sight of the larger picture. As always, my editor, Toby Sherry, offered the right balance of criticism, compassion, humor, and patience as this book went through its many drafts. My continued gratitude to my agent, Faith Hamlin, for her inimitable humor and belief in my work.

INTRODUCTION

In 1988, while researching a documentary history on American women, I found a memoir written in English by Zitkala-Ša (zit-KAH-
lah-shah), a Yankton woman who lived from 1876 to 1938. Her words
were so powerful, I set out to learn more about her. I discovered that
Zitkala-Ša means Red Bird. I learned that her birth name was Gertrude.
I found other words of hers in letters, speeches, poems, and traditional
stories. Her writings taught me much about the struggles of Native
Americans born after their people were confined to reservations. Her
honesty and relentless determination drew me to her.

I traveled to the Yankton Reservation in South Dakota where she
was born. I met her eighty-three-year-old niece and heard family stories. I learned that she had been born to a Yankton woman named
Taté Iyóhiwin, which means Every Wind, and a white man named
Felker. I saw places connected with Zitkala-Ša's life. I stood on the
bluff where her mother's tipi had once been, and looked out at the
same early morning mist over the Missouri River that she had written
about.

I visited the Uintah Reservation in Utah where she had lived for
thirteen years, and was startled by how different its stark beauty was
from the rolling hills of the South Dakota prairie. I walked along the
creek on her former ranch and on the site of the Indian boarding school
where she had once taught. I went home and buried myself in libraries
and archives and discovered that she was regarded as one of the most
important Native American reformers in the early pan-Indian movement in the twentieth century. I knew I had to write about her.

◆ ◆ *Introduction* ◆ ◆

I decided that Zitkala-Ša's words would be the most powerful way of telling her life story, so I have created what I call an autobiographical biography. Where I could not find her descriptions of episodes in her life, I read accounts by others and interviewed people who knew her. I have tried to re-create events as I believe she experienced them. Where my research has led me to conclude that her memory was inaccurate, I have made adjustments based on this research. Therefore, some reminiscences, speeches, letters, and stories are produced exactly as originally written; others have been edited and shortened without changing their meanings. Some chapters have been reconstructed from her letters, fragmentary notes, and diary entries. Paragraphing, punctuation, and spelling changes have been made for readability.

The titles of chapters about Zitkala-Ša's years on the Yankton Reservation are given in Dakota, with translations in English, to indicate that these were the only years in her life that she was surrounded by her language. The remaining chapter titles are given solely in English to reflect the continuous struggle by her and all Native Americans forced to renounce their culture. In middle age she alternated between her birth name Gertrude and Zitkala-Ša. I have chosen to continue calling her Zitkala-Ša to reflect the fact that until the end of her life she worked to reassert her Indian identity.

Some of Zitkala-Ša's words and phrases may seem old-fashioned or melodramatic. Some of her words, such as "paleface," are now considered offensive to Indians and non-Indians. As much as possible, I have kept her language intact, for it evokes her world.

If Zitkala-Ša were alive today, I hope she would view me as a friend and collaborator who remained true to her spirit and intentions. I hope that her life inspires others as it has inspired me.

The Yankton Reservation
1876–1884

Wóniya Kin Tínta Kin Píyawanikiye: The Breath That Brings Life to the Prairie

Taté Iyóhiwin (Every Wind) pushed open the flap of her tipi to welcome and honor the daylight. Her daughter was playing quietly on her soft bed by the fire. Three years before, on February 22, 1876, her daughter had been born to her and her white husband and given the name Gertrude. Later in her life Gertrude would give herself another name, Zitkala-Ša, which means Red Bird.

Gertrude was Taté Iyóhiwin's ninth born from three unions with white men. Only five of her nine children had survived. Her three oldest sons, from her first marriage, were grown now and lived a few miles away on the reservation. David, who was now twelve, was from her second marriage, Gertrude from her third.

Last fall the Indian agent on the reservation had threatened that if she did not send David to a school hundreds of miles away, her food rations would be cut in half. She had nowhere else to get food, so she had signed the permission paper, even though she could not read it. David had been taken from her.

THE FLIGHT OF RED BIRD

She did not know when she would see him again, and she knew that one day Gertrude would also be taken away.

When the sun bathed more of the sky, Taté Iyóhiwin slipped a deerskin dress over Gertrude's head and moccasins on her feet. She had spent many months beading the intricate designs on the dress and the moccasins. When Gertrude was older, Taté Iyóhiwin would teach her the art of beadwork.

Mother and daughter walked to the edge of the bluff overlooking the river. The morning mist over the marsh had

Lakota girl, South Dakota, ca. 1900. (Courtesy of the Center for Western Studies, Augustana College, Sioux Falls, SD.)

burned away. The air was clear and still. The river rippled and glistened in the sun. The prairie was awakening from its winter slumber. Perhaps today the meadowlarks would return.

Taté Iyóhiwin led Gertrude down the dirt path on the bluff to the road that led to the Indian agency at Greenwood a half mile away. Today was issue day. Her kinspeople were hurrying in the same direction down the white man's scar to get their monthly food rations. The muddy road was deeply grooved from the weight of the metal wheels of the stagecoaches and freight wagons that frequented Greenwood. At the river's edge, where once only canoes had graced the shoreline, white men were loading wood cut from reservation trees onto a steamboat to sell to other white men.

Mother's and daughter's moccasined feet made no noise as they passed St. Paul's Church, but Taté Iyóhiwin averted her

St. Paul's Church, Yankton Reservation, ca. 1874. (Courtesy of the Center for Western Studies, Augustana College, Sioux Falls, SD.)

eyes from the building anyway. She didn't want the minister to see her and come out and corner her. She didn't want him telling her again that her people's ways were the ways of the devil but that she could be saved if she loved a slender white man with long hair and sorrowful eyes called Jesus.

As they neared Greenwood, the road was more crowded with wagons and people. In town, horses loaded down with pelts were tied to the railing outside the barbershop. After a morning of stiff bargaining, the fur traders were having their hairy faces trimmed. The *clonk* of anvils and the screech of buzz saws pierced the air. There was no silence in Greenwood. No one here ever heard the meadowlarks sing.

At the agency they took their place in line to get food. How different Taté Iyóhiwin's life was from her mother's and grandmother's. How different it had been before the white explorers and fur trappers and settlers came. How different it had been before the white men controlled her people and their land. Her mother had told her of the visit in 1804 by the explorers Meriwether Lewis and William Clark. On their expedition to the Pacific Ocean they had stopped at a Yankton village on the Missouri River in this place now called the Dakota Territory. The Yanktons (Ihánktunwan, or People of the End Village) belonged to the confederation of Plains Indians known as the Sioux. The two white men and their entourage were hospitably received.

During their stay a son was born to a Yankton headman. It was said that when the explorers saw the newborn, they wrapped him in an American flag and predicted that he would become a leader of his people. It was said that that infant grew into the man Struck-by-the-Ree.

Fifty-four years later, in 1858, Struck-by-the-Ree found himself and nine other Yankton headmen in Washington, D.C., reluctantly signing a treaty with representatives of the United States government. He put an X next to his name because his people could no longer resist. The white men were more powerful than they were. He signed even though he knew that this treaty would forever alter the lives of his children and grandchildren and great-grandchildren.

The Yankton tribal leaders signed over 11 million acres of their people's land. In exchange 430,000 acres of their remaining land was "reserved" for them to live on. The federal government promised that for fifty years it would provide food, livestock, lumber, plows, cash, and other services totaling $1.6 million. The Yanktons were rounded up and force marched from their homes to the reservation. When they arrived on the reservation, they were told they could not leave without a written pass.

But greedy white hunters had been allowed to cross the plains at will, and they had slaughtered the millions of buffalo that had been the chief source of food and shelter and clothing for Taté Iyóhiwin's people. The horizon, once darkened by these shaggy monarchs, was empty; the buffalo were gone forever. Now, without government food she and her people would starve.

The line moved slowly as the Indian agent doled out meager portions of beef, flour, sugar, and salt. Taté Iyóhiwin knew there might not be anything left when it was her turn. Too often when the monthly food rations arrived, the agent sold large amounts to the owner of the hotel in Greenwood.

When she finally received her food, the sun was high, almost past the top of the sky. She took Gertrude's hand and they headed toward the muddy scar, then up the dirt path of the bluff. The climb was steep, but Taté Iyóhiwin walked quickly, hoping that when they reached the top, they would hear meadowlarks singing.

Wóunspe Tokáheya:
First Lessons

When Gertrude was twenty-four, she wrote about her childhood in the magazine *Atlantic Monthly*. She indicted federal agents, missionaries, and teachers who had carried out government policies to force Indians to adopt the white way of life. "Becoming white" had brought her pain and humiliation. She did not temper her bitterness or soften her anger to please her white readers. She desperately wanted them to understand how their government had tried to destroy her people's culture.

My mother's wigwam stood at the base of some hills. A footpath wound its way gently down the sloping land till it reached the broad river bottom. Creeping through the long swamp grasses, it came out on the edge of the Missouri River.

Morning, noon, and evening my mother came to draw water from the muddy stream. I always stopped my play to run along with her. Often she was sad and silent. One day her lips were compressed into hard, bitter lines, and shadows fell under her black eyes as tears fell from them. I clung to her hand and begged to know what made her tears fall.

"Hush," she said, "you must never talk about my tears." She patted my head and said, "Now let me see how fast you can run today."

I was a wild little girl of seven. Loosely clad in a slip of brown buckskin, I tore away, my long black hair blowing in the breeze. A pair of soft moccasins on my feet, I was as free as the wind that blew my hair. My mother's pride was my wild freedom and my overflowing spirits, and she taught me no fear save that of intruding myself upon others.

Many paces ahead I stopped, panting for breath and laughing with glee, as my mother watched my every movement.

Returning to her, I tugged beside her with my hands on my makebelieve bucket. "Mother, when I am tall as my cousin Wah-ċáziwin (Yellow Flower Woman), you shall not have to come to the river for water. I will do it for you," I said.

With a strange tremor in her voice which I could not understand, she answered, "If the paleface does not take away from us this river." Mother bit her lips as she spoke.

"Mother, who is this bad paleface?"

Setting the pail of water on the ground, my mother stooped. Stretching her left hand out on the level with my eyes, she placed her other arm about me and pointed to the hill where my uncle and my only sister lay buried.

"We were once very happy. But the paleface stole our lands and forced us away. On the day we moved camp, your sister and uncle were very sick. Many others were ailing, but there was no help. We traveled many days and nights, but not in the grand happy way that we moved camp when I was a little girl. We were driven like a herd of buffalo. With every step your sister, who was not as large as you are now, shrieked with pain until she was hoarse with crying. She grew more and more feverish. Her little hands and cheeks were burning hot. Her little lips were parched, but she would not drink the water I gave her. Her throat was swollen and red.

"When we reached this country, on the first weary night she died. And soon your uncle died, leaving his wife and your cousin Waȟcáziwin."

My mother was silent the rest of the way home. Though I saw no tears in her eyes, I knew that was because I was with her. She seldom wept before me.

Gertrude's mother had been married to three different white men. It is not known why her first two marriages ended, but Gertrude told a friend that her mother left her father when she was an infant because he had "scolded" David. Gertrude never described the "scolding," only that it so angered her mother that she not only left him but refused to let Gertrude have his last name. She gave Gertrude the last name of her second husband, Simmons. Most likely the "scolding" was a beating, for physical punishment was unpardonable in Indian family life.

Tiyóśpaye: Social Unit

Gertrude lived in a large circular camp of tipis of families from the Ċaġu (Lung) clan. Her kinspeople formed a *tiyóśpaye*, and the adults were Gertrude's secondary or auxiliary parents. The federal government tried to destroy tribal unity and traditional life by breaking up the social units, by moving people from their tipi villages to houses scattered across the reservation. The Yanktons passed down their traditions despite strict government policies that controlled their lives.

When Gertrude was two, her eleven-year-old brother David was sent east to a boarding school in Virginia. His three-year absence left her alone with her mother and explains why she never mentioned David in describing her early years.

The morning meal was our quiet hour, when we were alone. At noon people who chanced by stopped to rest and to share our lunch, for they were sure of our hospitality.

Though I heard many strange experiences told by these wayfarers, I loved best the evening meal, when the old legends were told. When the sun hung low in the west, my mother sent me to invite the neighboring old men and women to eat with us. My mother used to say to me, as I was bounding away, "Wait a moment before you invite anyone. And remember, if other plans are being discussed, do not interfere."

Running all the way, I halted shyly at the entrances to the wigwams. Sometimes I stood long moments without saying a word. The old folks knew the meaning of my pauses and often coaxed my confidence by asking, "What do you seek, little granddaughter?"

"My mother invites you to our tipi this evening," I exploded, and breathed the freer afterward.

They gladly accepted. My mission done, I ran home, skipping and jumping with delight. Out of breath I told my mother almost the exact words of the answers to my invitation. Frequently she asked, "What were they doing when you entered their tipi?" This taught me to remember all I saw at a single glance. Often I told my mother my impressions without being questioned.

At the arrival of our guests I sat close to my mother and did not leave her side without first asking her consent. I ate my supper in quiet, listening patiently to the talk of the old people, wishing all the time that they would finish talking and begin the stories.

In Indian society, education was a community effort, and winter storytelling was one part of a child's education. Yankton elders passed their knowledge on orally. Gertrude learned her people's history by listening to the tribal historian recounting from memory the major events of the last hundred years. The elders told stories that explained how the natural world came to be and how relationships developed between human beings and spirits, human beings and the animal world. Children listened carefully, for their elders often asked them to repeat what they had heard.

Gertrude loved the Iktomi stories. Like the spider he was named after, Iktomi wove a web of trickery. From the hundreds of tales of his pranks, Gertrude learned right from wrong. Iktomi had many sides—he was foolish, greedy, helpful, imaginative. Many times his appetites led him to pursue the forbidden, and his actions often transformed the world.

As each in turn began to tell a legend, I watched the stars peep down on me. The increasing interest of the tale aroused me, and I sat up eagerly listening for every word. The old women made funny remarks and laughed so heartily that I could not help joining them.

The distant howling of a pack of wolves or the hooting of an owl frightened me, and I nestled into my mother's lap. She added some dry sticks to the open fire, and the bright flames leaped up into the faces of the old folks in the circle.

An elder began a story:

It was the Moon of the Changing Season (September). Soon the yellow grass would disappear into the earth until spring. Prairie Flower's kinspeople had packed up the tipis and the children and gone to hunt buffalo. Prairie

Flower and her husband, Cloud Elk, had stayed behind, for Cloud Elk had been injured on a recent hunt.

Their food supply had dwindled to nothing, so every morning when the sun rose to light the earth, Prairie Flower gathered seed fruit from wild roses to cook. One day while picking red berries off a thorny bush, she heard a distant noise of hoofbeats. She looked up and saw a man on a snow-white pony chasing a buffalo across the prairie. The buffalo was galloping across the treeless plain straight toward her. Prairie Flower's heart pounded. There was no place to hide. The buffalo was almost upon her. She shielded her head with her hands, hoping the shaggy beast would run past her. Suddenly it fell dead at her feet from the hunter's arrow.

"Who are you?" the hunter asked, dismounting his horse, but he did not wait for her reply. "Stay." He flourished his knife. "I shall reward you."

The stranger boasted of his unsurpassed skill with the knife as he slit the hide down the middle of the spine into one long piece. Never losing a moment in self-praise, he bragged of his generosity as he carved the meat. "I always give the choicest cuts to the sick and hungry," he said.

Prairie Flower looked up to the sky and silently thanked the Great Spirit for bringing this large-hearted man.

She watched the hunter pack the meat, piece by piece, on his snow-white pony. Then he mounted his steed.

"Take this." He smiled, tossing the tripe to Prairie Flower. "It will make a good soup." He galloped away.

His meager gift stunned Prairie Flower, but she made a delicious soup from it and her husband said he felt stronger after eating it. She told him about the stranger. Cloud Elk listened intently but said nothing.

The next day, while searching for seed fruit, she saw the stranger again on his white pony chasing another buffalo across the plain. Again he downed the shaggy beast and promised to give her the choicest cuts if she but stood near him as he carved. So she watched and listened to him boast of his strength and generosity, but as on the day before, she was rewarded only with tripe.

This time Prairie Flower grabbed his pony's reins as the hunter prepared to ride away. "You are a man of empty words who boasts of helping the sick and poor, but it is a lie," she shouted. "I will tell my husband that you are a liar. He is a medicine man, and he will sing and beat on his sacred drum and scare the buffalo away from you."

"Do not tell him," the stranger groaned. He whispered, "I fear only four things in the world—the drum, the flute, deer-hoof rattles, and the screech owl. If your husband keeps these things away from me, tomorrow and every day after that I will hunt buffalo for you." He gave Prairie Flower all the meat she could carry and galloped away.

When she told her husband what had happened, he

knew at once that the stranger was misusing some sacred gift. "Let us see if he fulfills his promise," he said.

When the hunter did not return the next day, Cloud Elk stretched an old buffalo hide over a wooden frame and made a drum. From a long, straight piece of pine he carved a flute. He packed his deer-hoof rattles along with the drum and flute in a buckskin sack, and the couple set out across the prairie searching for The Man of Empty Words.

A day's journey away, on the other side of a forest of pine, they saw a lone tipi. They took their places on either side of the entrance. Prairie Flower shook the rattle and blew upon the flute, and Cloud Elk beat the sacred drum and hooted like an owl.

Out of the tipi into the thick woods ran The Man of Empty Words. His hands were pressed over his ears trying to stop the sounds from overwhelming him.

Prairie Flower pulled open the tipi flap, and they peered into the cone-shaped dwelling. All along its walls were large bags decorated with beads and porcupine quills. They opened the bags and saw that they were filled with dried meats and fruits and roots.

On a tall pole in the center of the tipi hung a large buffalo bladder. Its tough, wrinkled skin was embroidered with bright-colored porcupine quills. The bag was tied at the neck with the sinews of a moose.

"What an unusual bag," said Cloud Elk, for only un-decorated bags were used for food. He walked around

the bag and read the symbols on it. "I believe this is a sacred object," he whispered. "Perhaps as old as the beginning of the world. We must not touch it."

The couple passed the winter in the tipi and ate well. Cloud Elk became strong again, but he was troubled by the hanging bag. Sometimes it swayed to and fro upon the string when there was no wind blowing outside. At such times a tumultuous murmur came from within, and they heard the sound of hoofbeats, the rumble of trampling herds, the bellowing of buffalo, and the neighing of horses. Distant shouts of men and women rose above the rattle of drums and the clatter of gourds. Dogs barked and coyotes howled and the earth beneath the bag trembled. Cloud Elk and Prairie Flower sat in profound awe and burned sweet herbs in smoke prayers to the Great Mysterious Spirit.

In the Moon of the Red Grass Appearing (April), the food bags were empty. "Tomorrow we will return to our people to hunt with them," Cloud Elk said.

Just before the sun dipped low to touch the earth, Prairie Flower went to the forest to gather firewood. When she picked up a decaying log, she saw The Man of Empty Words hiding under it.

"Do not harm me!" he shrieked. "Listen! When you are out of meat, open the hanging bag in the tipi a little way and a buffalo will come out. Open it a little further and a white pony will emerge. Close it immediately. Tell your husband to mount the pony and chase the buffalo. Do as I say and you will always have meat."

Prairie Flower looked quickly about the forest to see if any person or animal had heard this sacred secret, but all was still. She turned back to the man again and saw nothing but an artichoke weed where he had stood. She returned to the tipi and told her husband what she had learned.

"We will open the sacred bag and see if what he said is true," said Cloud Elk. They took the bag down from the pole, carried it outside, and opened it a bit. Out jumped a buffalo. Prairie Flower opened the bag a little more, and a white pony appeared. Immediately she re-tied the bag. Cloud Elk mounted the pony and chased and killed the buffalo. It was the most savory, tender meat they had ever eaten.

"At daybreak," Cloud Elk said, "I will go by pony to invite our kinspeople to feast with us." He tied the white steed to a pole outside.

But when dawn streaked the sky, the loop at the end of the rope where the horse's neck had been was empty. Cloud Elk set out to their people on foot.

That evening, when the sun reached back down to touch the earth, an old man appeared at the tipi door. Prairie Flower recognized Iktomi, master of mischief. Without thinking, she told him of the contents of the sacred bag.

Iktomi walked around the buffalo bladder. "I am going to open that bag," he said.

"Please do not touch it," Prairie Flower pleaded, but Iktomi carried the pouch outside. In his greed to get at

its contents, he hastily untied the neck of the bag and dropped it to the ground. It fell wide open. Out surged a herd of buffalo, a herd so vast in number, one could not count them. They stampeded by in a mad fury. Bellowing and roaring with the voice of thunder, they trampled upon Iktomi and Prairie Flower and the tipi. The earth shook under their hoofs, and for as many miles as the prairie stretched west, it was blackened with shaggy beasts. And this, they say, is how the buffalo came to live on the great western plains.

The glare of the fire shone on a tattooed star on the brow of the old man who had told the story. The blue star was a puzzle to me. Looking about, I saw two parallel blue lines on the chin of an old woman. The rest of the women had none. I examined my mother's face but found no sign there. When the story was finished, I asked the old woman the meaning of the blue lines on her chin, looking all the while out of the corners of my eyes at the man with the star on his forehead. I was a little afraid he would rebuke me for my boldness.

The old woman said, "Why, my grandchild, they are signs—secret signs I dare not tell you. But I shall tell you a wonderful story about a woman who had a cross tattooed upon each of her cheeks."

It was a long story of a woman whose magic power lay hidden behind the marks on her face. I fell asleep before it was completed.

Wínyan: Woman

Gertrude's mother prepared her to be a traditional Yankton woman. She showed her where the wild turnips, cherries, and plums grew on the prairie and how to preserve meat and fruit. She taught her the art of beadwork, which became a lifelong pleasure for Gertrude.

Often after breakfast Mother began her beadwork. On a clear day she pulled out the wooden pegs that pinned the skirt of our wigwam to the ground and rolled the canvas partway up on its frame of slender poles. The cool morning breezes swept freely through our dwelling, now and then bringing the perfume of sweet grasses from newly burned prairie.

Untying the long tasseled strings of a small brown buckskin bag, my mother spread bunches of colored beads on a mat, as an artist arranges paints on a palette. On a lapboard she smoothed out a double sheet of soft white buckskin. From a beaded case hanging on her wide belt she drew a long, narrow blade and cut the buckskin. I felt my playmates' envious eyes on the pretty red-beaded moccasins that would soon decorate my feet.

I sat on a rug with a scrap of buckskin in one hand and an awl in the other and watched my mother. This was the beginning of my lessons in the art of beadwork. From a skein of finely twisted threads of silvery sinews, my mother pulled out a single one. With an awl she pierced the buckskin and skillfully threaded it with the white sinew. Picking up the tiny beads one by one, she strung them with the point of her thread, always twisting it carefully after every stitch. It took many trials before I learned how to knot my thread on the point of my finger as I saw her do.

The next difficulty was in keeping my thread stiffly twisted, so I could easily string my beads upon it. My mother insisted I make original designs. At first I spent many a sunny hour working a long design. Soon I learned not to draw complex patterns, for I had to finish whatever I began.

I usually drew simple crosses and squares. My original designs were not always symmetrical nor sufficiently characteristic, two faults with which my mother had little patience. She treated me as a dignified little individual as long as I was on my good behavior. I felt terribly humiliated when some boldness of mine drew forth a rebuke from her!

After these confining lessons I was wild with surplus spirits and found joyous relief in running with my playmates over the hills. Many a summer afternoon we each carried a sharpened rod about four feet long to pry up sweet roots. After eating the choice roots, we strayed off into patches of a stalky plant under whose yellow blossoms are found little crystal drops of gum. Drop by drop we gathered nature's rock candy until each of us had a lump the size of a small bird's egg. We chewed and chewed it. Soon, sated with its woody flavor, we tossed away our gum and returned to find more sweet roots.

We pretended to give each other our necklaces, beaded belts, and moccasins as gifts. We delighted in impersonating our mothers. We talked of things we had heard them say in their conversations. We imitated their various manners, even to the inflection of their voices. We seated ourselves, leaned our cheeks in the palms of our hands, rested our elbows on our knees, and bent forward as they did. When one of us told of some heroic deed recently done by a near relative, the rest of us listened attentively and exclaimed, "*Han! han!*" (Yes! yes!) whenever the speaker paused for breath or sympathy. As our discourse became more thrilling, our *Han! han!*s were louder and louder.

No matter how exciting the tale, the mere shifting of a cloud shadow in the landscape was sufficient to make us take off and chase it on the hills. We shouted and whooped in the chase, laughing and calling to one another as we ran along hoping to catch the shadow.

Wašíčun Kin Owéwakankan Táwapi: White Men's Lies

"Transfer the savage-born infant to civilization and he will develop a civilized language and habit. . . . Kill the Indian in him, and save the man," was the motto of Richard Henry Pratt, a captain in the U.S. Army.

Like most whites in the nineteenth century Pratt viewed Indian culture and education as worthless. He believed the only way to solve the "problem" of the "savage, uncivilized" Indian was to separate children from their kinspeople as early as possible and teach them "how to be white." Pratt's ideas took hold, and by 1884 there were forty-nine Indian boarding schools set up away from reservations. Recruiters took children as young as four.

The first turning away from the easy, natural flow of my life occurred in 1884, when I was eight. At this age I knew but one language, and that was my mother's native tongue. From my playmates I heard that two paleface missionaries were in our village. They said these men (Quakers) wore big hats and carried large hearts. I asked my mother why these strangers were among us. I pestered her until she told me that they had come to take away Indian boys and girls to the East. My mother did not seem to want me to talk about them.

Some parents, resigned to the fact that their way of life was quickly vanishing, believed their children needed to be educated in white ways. But they did not want their young ones leaving them, even to go to boarding schools on the reservations. Federal agents tried persuasion. If that didn't work, food rations were withheld. To keep their other children from starving, parents gave in. Some parents hid their children, but the agency police tracked them down and dragged them out from their hiding places. Sometimes children were kidnapped and for months parents were frantic, not knowing where they had been taken.

I heard wonderful stories about the strangers from my friend Judéwin. I told Mother, "Judéwin is going home with the missionaries to a more beautiful country than ours. The palefaces told her so!" I wished in my heart that I too might go.

Three years ago my brother David had returned from Hampton Normal Institute, an industrial training school in Virginia. His coming back influenced my mother to take a step from her native way of living. First it was a change from the buffalo-skin covering of our wigwam to the white man's canvas. Recently she had given up her wigwam of slender poles to live like a foreigner in a home of clumsy logs.

"Yes, my child, several others besides Judéwin are going away with the palefaces. Your brother said they had inquired about you." My heart thumped so hard, I wondered if she could hear it.

"Did he tell them to take me, Mother?" I asked, fearing that David had forbidden the missionaries to see me and that my hope of going to the Wonderland would be blighted.

With a sad, slow smile she answered, "Judéwin has filled your ears with the white men's lies. Don't believe a word they say. Their words are sweet, my child, but their deeds are bitter. Stay with me, my little one! David says that going East will be too hard for his baby sister."

The following day I spied the missionaries coming up the foot-path to our house. A young interpreter, who had a smattering of our language, was with them. I was ready to run out to meet them, but I did not dare displease my mother. I jumped up and down on the floor. I begged my mother to open the door so they would be sure to come to us.

When they came in, they smiled into my eyes and patted my head. I wondered how Mother could say such hard words against these kind strangers.

Judéwin had told me that they lived in the East, in a land of great trees filled with red, red apples. You could reach out your hands and pick all the red apples you could eat there. I had never seen apple trees. I had never tasted more than a dozen red apples in my life. I was eager to see these orchards.

"Mother, ask them if little girls may have all the red apples they want when they go East," I whispered aloud.

The interpreter answered, "Yes, little girl, the nice red apples are for those who pick them. And you will ride on the iron horse if you go with these good people."

I had never seen a train, and he knew it.

"Mother, I like big red apples, and I want to ride on the iron horse. Mother, say yes!" I pleaded.

My mother said nothing. The missionaries waited in silence. My eyes began to blur with tears, though I struggled to choke them back. The corners of my mouth twitched. Mother told the missionaries that she would give them her answer tomorrow.

They left us. Alone with my mother, I yielded to my tears, shaking my head so as not to hear what she said to me. This was the first time I had been so unwilling to give up my own desire that I refused to listen to my mother. There was a solemn silence in our home that night. Before I went to bed, I begged the Great Spirit to make my mother let me go.

The next morning my dear aunt came to the house. I hoped that as usual my aunt was pleading on my behalf.

My mother called me to her side. "Do you still persist in wishing to leave your mother?" she asked.

"Mother, it is not that I wish to leave you, but I want to see the wonderful Eastern land."

My aunt said, "Let her try it."

Mother turned to my aunt. "But she does not understand what it all means. I know she will suffer keenly in this experiment, so I dread letting her go."

A few days later, wrapped in my heavy blanket, I walked with my mother to the carriage that would take us to the iron horse.

I was happy. My playmates were also wearing their best thick blankets. We showed one another our new beaded moccasins and the width of the belts around our new dresses. There were eight in our party—three young boys, two tall girls, Judéwin, our friend Totówin, and I. We dreamed of roaming as freely and happily under a sky of rosy apples as we had chased the cloud shadows on the Dakota plains.

At most partings both children and parents wept uncontrollably. Gertrude went willingly, seduced by the promise of the Red Apple Country. For the past two years she had attended a reservation day school. Her classes had been taught in her language, and each evening she had returned home. Despite being warned, Gertrude had no idea what life would be like at boarding school, or that the school was over 700 miles from home.

Red Apple Country
1884–1887

The Journey

Almost immediately after leaving her mother, Gertrude felt frightened and puzzled by the strange world around her.

When the horses drew us rapidly away, I saw the lonely figure of my mother vanish in the distance and a sense of regret settled heavily upon me. I felt suddenly weak, as if I might fall limp to the ground. I was with strangers whom my mother did not fully trust. I no longer felt free to be myself or to voice my own feelings. Tears trickled down my cheeks, and I buried my face in the folds of my blanket.

We were told the Red Apple Country lay a little beyond the great circular horizon of the Western prairie. We anticipated much pleasure from a ride on the iron horse.

On the train, fair women with tottering babies on each arm stared at us. Large men with heavy bundles in their hands riveted their eyes upon us. I sank deep into the corner of my seat, for I resented being watched. Children no larger than I stared at us too. Sometimes they took their fingers out of their mouths and pointed at my moccasined feet. Their mothers did not scold them for their rudeness. Instead the mothers looked closely at me and attracted their children's further notice to my blanket. This embarrassed me and kept me constantly on the verge of tears.

I sat perfectly still, with my eyes downcast, daring only now and then to look around me. Chancing to turn to a window, I was breathless on seeing a familiar object—a telegraph pole. Very near my mother's house, along the edge of a road thickly bordered with wild sunflowers, some poles like these had been planted by white men. Often I had held my ear against these poles and heard their low moaning and wondered what the palefaces had done to hurt the poles. Now I sat watching for each pole, temporarily forgetting my uncomfortable surroundings.

We rode several days inside the iron horse.

It was night when we reached the grounds of White's Manual Labor Institute in Wabash, Indiana. The wagon pulled up in front of a massive brick building. The lights from its windows fell upon some of the icicled trees that stood beneath them. We were led toward an open door where the brightness of the lights within flooded out. My body trembled.

Once we were inside, the glaring light in the large, whitewashed hall dazzled my eyes. The noisy hurrying of hard shoes on the bare wooden floor increased the whirring in my ears. My only safety seemed to be keeping next to the wall.

As I was wondering how to escape from all this confusion, two warm hands grasped me firmly and tossed me up in the air. A rosy-cheeked woman caught me in her arms. I was both frightened and insulted by such trifling. I stared into her eyes, wishing her to let me stand on my own feet, but she jumped me up and down with increasing enthusiasm. My mother had never made a plaything of me. Remembering this, I began to cry aloud.

The woman misunderstood why I was crying and placed me at a table loaded with food. As I did not stop crying, one of the older Indian girls at the table whispered to me, "Wait until you are alone."

"I want my mother and my brother. I want my aunt!" I pleaded in my language, but the ears of the palefaces could not hear me.

We were taken up an incline of wooden boxes, which I later learned to call a stairway. At the top was a quiet, dimly lighted hall. Many narrow beds, with sleeping brown faces peeping out of the coverings, lined the wall. I was tucked into bed with one of the tall girls. She talked to me in my mother tongue, and it soothed me.

I had arrived in the wonderful land of rosy skies, but I was not happy, as I had thought I would be. My long travel and the bewildering sights had exhausted me.

I fell asleep, heaving deep, tired sobs. My tears were left to dry themselves in streaks, because neither my aunt nor my mother was there to wipe them away.

The First Day at School

The first day in the land of red apples was a bitter-cold one. Snow still covered the ground, and the trees were bare. A large bell rang for breakfast, its loud metallic voice crashing through the belfry overhead into our sensitive ears several hours before sunrise. The annoying clatter of shoes gave us no peace. The constant clash of harsh noises, with many voices murmuring an unknown tongue, made a bedlam within which I was securely tied. And though my spirit tore itself in struggling for its lost freedom, all was useless.

A woman with white hair came for us. We were placed in a line with other Indian girls dressed in stiff shoes and closely clinging dresses. The small girls wore sleeved aprons and had shingled (close-cropped and layered) hair.

I felt like sinking to the floor, for my blanket had been stripped from my shoulders. I looked hard at the Indian girls who had been here awhile. They seemed not to care that they were even more immodestly dressed than I in their tight-fitting clothes.

In the dining room I spied the three boys from home, looking as uncomfortable as I felt.

A small bell was tapped and each pupil drew a chair from under the table. I assumed this meant we should sit, so I pulled out my chair and slipped into it. But when I turned my head, I saw I was the only one seated. I rose, looking shyly around to see how the chairs were to be used, when a second bell

Students at White's, 1886. Gertrude is third from left in front row. (Courtesy of White's Residential and Family Services, Inc.)

sounded. All were seated at last. I had to crawl back into my chair again. I heard a man's voice at one end of the hall and looked around to see him. All the others' heads were bent over their plates.

As I glanced at the long chain of tables, I caught the eyes of a paleface woman upon me. Immediately I dropped my eyes, wondering why I was so keenly watched by the strange woman. The man ceased his mutterings and a third bell was tapped.

Everyone picked up his knife and fork and began eating. I began crying instead, for by this time I was afraid to venture anything more.

Later in the morning Judéwin gave me a terrible warning. She knew a few words of English and had overheard the woman talk about cutting our long hair. Our mothers had taught us that only unskilled warriors who were captured had their hair shingled by the enemy. Among our people short hair was worn by mourners, and shingled hair by cowards.

We discussed our fate some moments, and Judéwin said, "We have to submit, because they are strong."

"No, I will not submit! I will struggle first!" I answered.

I watched for my chance, and when no one noticed, I disappeared. I crept up the stairs as quietly as I could in my squeaking shoes—for after breakfast my moccasins had been taken from me and exchanged for shoes.

I did not know where I was going. Turning aside to an open door, I saw into a large room with three beds. The windows were covered with dark-green curtains, which made the room dim. I crawled under the bed and cuddled myself in the dark corner.

From my hiding place I peered out, shuddering with fear whenever I heard footsteps nearby. In the hall loud voices were calling my name. I knew that even Judéwin was searching for me. I did not open my mouth to answer.

The steps quickened and the voices became excited. The sounds came nearer and nearer. Women and girls entered the room. I held my breath and watched them open closet doors and peep behind large trunks. Someone threw up the curtains, and the room was filled with sudden light.

What caused them to stoop and look under the bed I do not know. I remember being dragged out, though I resisted by kicking and scratching wildly. I was carried downstairs and tied fast in a chair.

I cried aloud, shaking my head all the while until I felt the cold blades of the scissors against my neck and heard them gnaw off one of my thick braids. Then I lost my spirit. Since I had been taken from my mother, I had suffered extreme indignities. People had stared at me. I had been tossed about in the air like a wooden puppet. And now my long hair was being shingled like a coward's. I moaned for my mother, but no one came to comfort me. Not a soul reasoned quietly with me, as my mother would have done. For now I was only one of many little animals driven by a herder.

"Killing the Indian" in Gertrude had begun. Within twenty-four hours she was stripped of things that defined her identity—her blanket, her soft moccasins, her hair, her language. Children with Indian names were given Euro-American names and forbidden to ever utter the names their parents had given them. Gertrude was humiliated, frightened, and confused. At home she had been surrounded by a loving, caring community. Now she was alone in a strange environment ruled by bells, an unknown language, and foreign ways.

Loneliness haunted her and the other children. Many youngsters cried themselves to sleep every night; many tossed and turned but found no sleep. They wet their beds, stopped eating, and developed chronic stomachaches and diarrhea. Some children wrote their parents begging to come home. It required great ingenuity to get such a letter posted, for the teachers censored outgoing mail.

Worried parents protested to the Indian agent: No one had told them that their child would be away for up to five years when they signed the permission paper. They begged for their children to come home for at least short vacations; it was rarely allowed.

"No!"

A short time after our arrival Judéwin, Totówin, and I played outside in the snowdrifts. We were still deaf to the English language, except Judéwin. That morning we learned through her ears that we were forbidden to fall lengthwise in the snow as we had been doing, to see our impressions. However, before many hours we had forgotten the order and were having wonderful sport in the snow when a shrill voice called us inside. We shook the snow off ourselves and walked slowly toward the woman.

Judéwin said, "The paleface is angry with us. She is going to punish us for falling into the snow. If she looks straight into your eyes and talks loudly, you must wait until she stops. Then, after a tiny pause, say, 'No.'" The rest of the way we practiced the little word "no."

Totówin was summoned into the room for judgment first. The door shut behind her with a click. Judéwin and I listened at the keyhole. The woman talked in severe tones. Her words fell from her lips like crackling embers, and her inflection was like the end of a switch. I understood her voice better than the things she was saying. I was certain we had made her very impatient.

"Oh, poor Totówin!" Judéwin gasped. She understood enough of the woman's words to realize that she had taught us the wrong reply.

Just then I heard Totówin's tremulous answer, "No."

With an angry exclamation the woman spanked Totówin hard. "Are you going to obey me the next time?" she asked again.

Totówin answered with the only English word she knew, "No."

This time the woman meant her blows to smart, for Totówin shrieked at the top of her voice. In the midst of the whipping the blows ceased abruptly. "Are you going to fall in the snow again?" the woman asked.

Totówin answered feebly, "No, no."

The door opened. The woman led Totówin out, stroking her black shorn head. She did nothing to Judéwin or to me.

During the first two or three seasons misunderstandings as ridiculous as this one frequently took place, bringing unjustifiable frights and punishments into our little lives.

Indian parents taught by example, not by physical punishment. Breaking rules in boarding school led to punishments ranging from ridicule to whippings. In many schools children who wet their beds were made to carry their mattresses around with them all day. Children caught speaking their native language or performing ceremonies might be made to stand on tiptoe with their arms outstretched for an hour or two or three. Disobedient girls were often ordered to lift their dresses while they were paddled in front of their classmates.

A boy who ran away might be forced to wear a girl's dress, or be whipped with a rubber hose or made to walk with a ball and chain around his ankles. Some boys were locked to their beds at night. Three boys ran away during Gertrude's stay at White's. School records state that when they were found, they were "kept in a safe place where they had nothing to do but reflect on the error of their ways." Most likely they were kept in a dark basement, with a bucket in the room for a toilet and fed only bread and water, for that was common punishment in boarding schools for runaways.

Within a year I was able to express myself somewhat in broken English. As soon as I comprehended a part of what was said and done, a mischievous spirit of revenge possessed me.

One day I was called in from my play for some misconduct. I had disregarded a rule which seemed to me very needlessly binding and was sent into the kitchen to mash the turnips for dinner. I hated turnips and their odor. With fire in my heart I took the wooden tool that the woman held out to me. I stood upon a step, and grasping the handle with both hands, I bent in hot rage over the turnips.

I worked my vengeance upon them. Everyone else in the kitchen was so busily occupied that no one noticed me. Soon I saw that the turnips were in a pulp and that further beating would not improve them. But the order had been "Mash these turnips," and mash I would! I renewed my energy. And as I sent the masher into the bottom of the jar, I felt a satisfying sensation that the weight of my body had gone into it.

One of the matrons came up to my table. She looked into the jar and shoved my hands roughly aside. I stood fearless and angry. She placed her red hands upon the rim of the jar. She lifted it and moved away from the table. The pulpy contents fell through the broken glass at the bottom of the jar to the floor. The woman spared me no scolding phrases that I had earned. I did not heed them. I felt triumphant in my revenge, though deep within me I was a wee bit sorry to have broken the jar.

As I sat eating my dinner and saw that no turnips were served, I whooped in my heart for having once asserted the rebellion within me.

White's was run like a military camp. At five A.M. the bells began ringing, and they didn't stop until bedtime. Roll call followed wake-up to assure that no one had run away during the night. Then beds were made, clothes were donned, and nightshirts were neatly folded under the pillow. With the next bell the children marched off to breakfast, then more bells and on to religious worship.

White's was an elementary school with four grades. From December through April classes began at seven A.M. and lasted until three P.M. Every student was expected to learn to read, speak, and write English. The Bible was a daily textbook. The children studied geography, U.S. history, elocution, physiology, and arithmetic. But the real work of the school was to train the boys as farmers and the girls as proper homemakers for their future farmer husbands. Once planting season began, boys under twelve spent only half a day in the classroom, the older boys only ninety minutes.

The federal government never provided enough money or staff to run the boarding schools, so the superintendents put the children to work to make up the difference. The older boys tended the livestock and grew enough food to feed students and faculty. They also repaired buildings and fences.

Barn complex at White's, ca. 1884. (Courtesy of White's Residential and Family Services, Inc.)

The girls sewed clothing and bedding. In hot, unventilated laundries they bent over washboards, rubbing and rubbing until not one speck of dirt was left on any item. Sheets, blouses, tablecloths, and curtains were ironed until faultlessly smooth. Some girls were assigned to scrub floors and stairs and walls. Others milked the cows or plucked the feathers from the chickens and turkeys, then roasted the birds and baked apple pies.

There was no rest after dinner. Instead there were lectures against drinking and gambling, or talks on American history and government, or readings from popular novels like *Black Beauty*. On Saturdays there were music lessons and brass-band rehearsal. For the younger children the day ended at seven-thirty P.M. The older children didn't stop until nine P.M.

Going home to see parents was forbidden, but for months at a time children were sent to live with families in nearby towns to learn how "real" families functioned. In most homes the children were treated like servants.

Hoping to get additional money, school officials paraded the students before the community and the politicians to show how the school had transformed these "little savages." Forbidden to perform their own religious ceremonies, the children were nevertheless made to perform "native" dances at local arts-and-crafts fairs. They were taken to temperance meetings, where they stood up and pledged never to drink or smoke tobacco.

The Stories of the Bible

Most whites had no understanding of the complex religious traditions of the Indians and believed that Indians had to be converted to Christianity if they were ever to become "civilized." As the federal government gained more control over the lives of Native Americans, it outlawed Indian healing and spiritual religious practices.

Students at White's were compelled to attend morning prayers in English and to read Bible stories. Many of these stories baffled and frightened Gertrude.

Among the legends the elders used to tell me were stories of evil spirits, but I was taught not to fear them any more than those spirits who stalked about in material guise. I never knew there was an insolent chieftain among the bad spirits, who dared to array his forces against the Great Spirit, until I heard this legend from a paleface woman.

Out of a large book she showed me a picture of the white man's devil. I looked in horror upon the strong claws that grew out of his fur-covered fingers. His feet were like his hands. Trailing at his heels was a scaly tail tipped with a serpent's open jaws. His face was a patchwork; he had bearded cheeks. His nose was like an eagle's bill, and his sharp-pointed ears were pricked up like those of a sly fox. Above them a pair of cow's horns curved upward. I trembled with awe, and my heart throbbed in my throat as I looked at the king of evil spirits. The woman said that this terrible creature roamed loose in the world, and that little girls who disobeyed school regulations would be tortured by him.

That night I dreamed about this evil divinity. I was in my mother's house. An Indian woman had come visiting. On opposite sides of the kitchen stove, which stood in the center of the small house, my mother and her guest sat in straight-backed chairs. I played with a train of empty spools hitched together on a string. It was night, and the wick burned feebly. Suddenly I heard the doorknob turn from without.

My mother and the woman hushed their talk and looked toward the door. I waited behind the stove. The hinges squeaked as the door was slowly pushed inward.

In rushed the devil! He looked exactly like the picture in the book. He did not speak to my mother, because he did not know our language, but his glittering yellow eyes fastened upon me. He took long strides around the stove, passing behind the woman's chair. I threw down my spools and ran to my mother. He followed closely after me. I ran round and round the stove, crying aloud for help.

My mother and the woman seemed not to know my danger. They sat still, looking quietly upon the devil's chase after me. I grew dizzy. My knees became numb and doubled under my weight like a pair of knife blades without a spring. I fell in a heap beside my mother's chair. Just as the devil stooped over me with outstretched claws, my mother awoke from her quiet indifference and lifted me on her lap. The devil vanished and I was awake.

The following morning I took my revenge upon the devil. I stole into the room with the wall of shelves filled with books. I drew forth *The Stories of the Bible*. With a broken slate pencil I began by scratching out his wicked eyes. When I left the room, there was a ragged hole in the page where his picture had been.

Once I lost a dear classmate. I remember well how she used to mope along at my side, until one morning she could not raise her head from her pillow. At her deathbed I stood weeping, as the paleface woman sat near her moistening the dry lips. Among the folds of the bedclothes I saw the open pages of the Bible. The dying Indian girl talked disconnectedly of Jesus the Christ and the woman who was cooling her swollen hands and feet.

I grew bitter, and censured the woman for cruel neglect of our physical ills. I despised the teaspoon which dealt out, from a large bottle, healing to a row of variously ailing Indian children. I blamed the hard-working, well-meaning ignorant woman who was inculcating into our hearts her superstitious ideas.

I was sullen in my troubles, but as soon as I felt better, I was ready again to smile upon the cruel woman. Within a week I was again actively testing the chains which tightly bound my individuality like a mummy for burial.

Indians had little resistance to European diseases, and contracting tuberculosis, measles, and smallpox meant death far more often than for whites. The long working hours at boarding school caused physical exhaustion, and restful sleep did not come easily with four or five children crammed into one bed. In one school seventy-five boys had to wash in the same water and share the same towels. They passed to each other contagious diseases such as trachoma, an eye infection that often led to blindness. There were no antibiotics then, and many children developed illnesses that lasted the rest of their lives.

During Gertrude's stay at White's, out of 203 students, 22 were sent home because of chronic health problems. Three died shortly after. Five children died at school. Their parents were not allowed to see them before they died, nor were their bodies returned home to be buried.

Between Two Worlds
1887–1902

The Returned Student

In 1887, after three years in Indiana, eleven-year-old Gertrude was allowed to return to her mother. Nineteen months later she was shipped off again to a boarding school on the Santee Reservation, thirty miles away in Nebraska, just across the

Pupils at Santee Normal Training School, ca. 1890. Gertrude is third from right in back row. (Courtesy of the Center for Western Studies, Augustana College, Sioux Falls, SD.)

THE FLIGHT OF RED BIRD

Missouri River. In June 1890 she returned home, a restless adolescent.

At White's, Gertrude had yearned for her mother and her kin, but reservation life no longer provided comfort and security. She felt isolated from her tribal culture and childhood friends. Nearing fifteen, she was in emotional turmoil, suspended between two cultures.

Back in the Western country, I hung in the heart of chaos, beyond the touch or voice of human aid. My brother David, being almost ten years my senior, did not quite understand my feelings. My mother had never gone inside a schoolhouse, so she was not capable of comforting her daughter who could read and write. Even nature seemed to have no place for me. I was neither a wee girl nor a tall one; neither a wild Indian nor a tame one. This deplorable situation was the effect of my time in the East, and the unsatisfactory "teenth" in a girl's years.

It was under these trying conditions that one bright afternoon, as I sat restless and unhappy in my mother's cabin, I caught the sound of the spirited step of my brother's pony on the road passing by our dwelling. Soon I heard the wheels of a light buckboard, and David's familiar "Ho!" to his pony. He alighted on the bare ground in front of our house. Tying his pony to one of the projecting corner logs of the low-roofed dwelling, he stepped on the wooden doorstep.

I met him there with a hurried greeting, and as I passed by, he looked a quiet "What?" into my eyes.

When he began talking with my mother, I slipped the rope

from the pony's bridle. Seizing the reins and bracing my feet against the dashboard, I wheeled around in an instant. The pony was ever ready to try his speed. Looking backward, I saw David waving his hand to me. I turned with the curve in the road and disappeared.

I followed the winding road which crawled upward between the bases of little hillocks. Deep water-worn ditches ran parallel on either side. A strong wind blew against my cheeks and fluttered my sleeves. The pony reached the top of the highest hill and began an even race on the level lands. There was nothing moving within that great circular horizon of the Dakota prairies, save the tall grasses over which the wind blew and rolled off in long, shadowy waves. In this vast wigwam of blue and green, I rode reckless and insignificant. It satisfied my small consciousness to see the white foam fly from the pony's mouth.

Suddenly, out of the earth, a coyote came forth. Upon the moment's impulse, I gave him a long chase and a wholesome fright. As I turned away to go back to the village, the coyote sank down upon his haunches to rest, for it was a hot summer day. And as I drove slowly homeward, I saw his sharp nose still pointed at me, until I vanished below the margin of the hilltops.

In a little while I came in sight of my mother's house. David stood in the yard, laughing at an old man who was pointing his forefinger and waving his hand toward the hills. With his blanket drawn over one shoulder, the old man talked and motioned excitedly. David turned the old man by the shoulder and pointed to me.

"*Oh han!*" ("Oh yes!") the man muttered, and went his way.

THE FLIGHT OF RED BIRD

He had climbed the top of his favorite hill to survey the surrounding prairies when he spied my chase after the coyote. His keen eyes recognized the pony and driver. Uneasy for my safety, he had come running to my mother's cabin to give her warning. I did not appreciate his kindly interest, for there was an unrest gnawing at my heart.

As soon as the man went away, I asked David if I could join him that evening at a party.

"No, my baby sister, I cannot take you with me to the party," he answered. I was not far from fifteen, and I felt that before long I should enjoy all the privileges of my tall cousin, but David persisted in calling me his baby sister.

That moonlit night I cried in my mother's presence when I heard David and his friends pass by our cottage. They were no more young men in blankets and eagle plumes, nor Indian maids with prettily painted cheeks. They had gone to school in the East and had become civilized. The young men wore the white man's coat and trousers with bright neckties. The girls wore tight muslin dresses, with ribbons at neck and waist. At these gatherings they talked English. I could speak English almost as well as my brother, but I was not properly dressed to be taken along. I had no hat, no ribbons, and no close-fitting gown. Since my return from school I had thrown away my shoes and again wore soft moccasins.

My mother was troubled by my unhappiness. She offered me the only printed matter we had in our home, a Bible given to her some years ago by a missionary. She tried to console me. "Here, my child, are the white man's papers. Read a little from them," she said most piously.

I took it from her hand, for her sake; but my enraged spirit felt more like burning the book, which offered me no help and was a perfect delusion to my mother. I did not read it. I laid it unopened on the floor, where I sat on my feet. The dim yellow light of the braided muslin burning in a small vessel of oil flickered and sizzled in my awful silent storm.

My wrath against the fates consumed my tears before they reached my eyes. I sat stony, with a bowed head. My mother threw a shawl over her head and shoulders and stepped out into the night.

After an uncertain solitude, I was suddenly aroused by a loud cry piercing the night. It was my mother's voice wailing among the barren hills which held the bones of buried warriors. She called aloud for her brothers' spirits to support her in her helpless misery. My fingers grew icy cold, as I realized that my unrestrained tears had betrayed my suffering to her, and she was grieving for me.

When she ceased her weeping and I knew she would return to our dwelling, I extinguished the light and leaned my head on the windowsill.

Schemes of running away hovered about in my mind. A few more moons of such turmoil drove me back to the Eastern school. I rode on the iron steed, thinking it would bring me back to my mother in a few winters, when I should be grown tall, and there would be friends awaiting me.

Gertrude felt suspended between two worlds, between the old ways and the new ways. This was a common feeling among returned students. Some tried to resolve their confusion by taking up traditional life again, wearing Indian garb and speaking their native language. Others straddled both worlds, working for the Indian Service as teachers, clerks, interpreters, or police officers. Many died prematurely from diseases contracted at boarding school. Others sank into depression and alcoholism.

On December 15, 1890, the great Sioux leader Sitting Bull was murdered by Indian police sent to arrest him. Fourteen days later, on December 29, over 300 Sioux men, women, and children were massacred at Wounded Knee in South Dakota. Black Elk, a holy man who witnessed the massacre, believed that something besides people died at Wounded Knee: "A people's dream died there. . . . The nation's hoop was broken and scattered."

In February 1891, four years after leaving White's, Gertrude returned, hoping to quell her uncertainty and pain. She asked a tribal holy man for sacred herbs to assure her of making friends. She wore them in a buckskin bag around her neck until she lost the bag a year later.

Though she resisted being turned into a carbon-copy white girl, school records reveal that Gertrude loved learning and was an exceptional student. She had a flair for dramatics and used her storytelling gifts to master the art of public speaking, an essential part of education then. To the music teacher's delight she had a beautiful singing voice and became an accomplished violinist and pianist. When the music teacher resigned, Gertrude took over her classes, even though she was still a student. When the bookkeeper left, she took over that job too.

Having been trained by her elders to listen and remember, she easily memorized the names, dates, and important facts in American history. She appreciated the energy and achievements of the century-old nation despite its brutality toward the Indians. She learned that the new settlers had exploited other peoples. Her Quaker teachers told her of the slave uprisings that mirrored the armed conflicts of Indians. She learned that women had been at the forefront of the abolitionist movement to end slavery, defying the idea that it was improper for them to speak in public. At Quaker meetings Gertrude heard effective women speakers. Now many women were involved in campaigns to prohibit alcohol, and gain the vote for women.

In 1893 school officials sent seventeen-year-old Gertrude and another Indian student on recruiting trips to South Dakota. On one trip they brought back twenty-nine children from the Pine Ridge Reservation. Gertrude's schooling had so successfully "killed the Indian" in her that she now served as the *wašíčun*'s agent, separating Indian children from their parents. She had successfully buried the pain and sadness she had felt when she had left her mother at eight years old.

Two years later, on June 28, 1895, citizens of Wabash and neighboring towns gathered on the school lawn for commencement. The graduates sang, recited poetry, and gave speeches. Nineteen-year-old Gertrude boldly tackled the subject of the inequality of women in a nation that prided itself on equality. "Half of humanity cannot rise while the other half is in subjugation," she declaimed. "When women are kept down, men must necessarily occupy the same level." The Wabash *Times* called her speech "a masterpiece that has never been surpassed in eloquence or literary perfection by any girl in this county."

A Quaker woman offered to pay Gertrude's tuition at Earlham College, a Quaker school in Richmond, Indiana. Gertrude accepted. She had the summer off, but did not choose to return home even though she had not seen her mother in four years. She stayed in Wabash and taught music to young children.

Two Contests

In the autumn of 1895 I ventured upon a college career against my mother's will. I had written for her approval, but in her reply I found no encouragement. She reminded me that her neighbors' children had completed their education in three years. They had returned home and were talking English with the frontier settlers. My mother's few words hinted that I had better give up my slow attempt to learn the white man's ways and be content to come home. I silenced her by deliberate disobedience.

Gertrude's brother David, and his wife, Victoria, now lived on the reservation. David worked there as a clerk for the Bureau of Indian Affairs. It is not known what David thought of Gertrude's decision to go to college, but Victoria disapproved. She wrote Gertrude that she was deserting home and suggested that if she continued on this path, she should give up the family name. Victoria's disapproval pained Gertrude, but it did not stop her from going to college.

THE FLIGHT OF RED BIRD

Homeless and heavy-hearted, I began my life among strangers. As I hid myself in my little room in the college dormitory, away from the scornful and yet curious eyes of the students, I pined for sympathy. Often I wept in secret, wishing I had gone West, to be nourished by my mother's love, instead of remaining among a cold race whose hearts were frozen hard with prejudice.

During the fall and winter seasons I scarcely had a real friend, though by that time several of my classmates were courteous to me at a safe distance.

My mother had not yet forgiven my rudeness to her, and I had no time for letter writing. By daylight and lamplight I spun with reeds and thistles, until my hands were tired from their weaving, the magic design which promised the white man's respect.

In January 1896, five months into my first year at Earlham, I entered our school oratorical contest. In the chapel the classes assembled with their invited guests. The high platform was carpeted and gaily festooned with college colors. A bright white light illumined the room and outlined clearly the great polished beams that arched the domed ceiling. The assembled crowds filled the air with pulsating murmurs. When the hour for speaking arrived, all were hushed, but on the wall the old clock which pointed out the trying moment ticked calmly on.

One after another I heard the orators. I could not realize that they longed for the favorable decision of the judges as much as I did. Each contestant received a loud burst of applause, and some were cheered heartily. Too soon my turn came. I paused a moment behind the curtains for a deep breath.

The child Gertrude had listened carefully as the elder storytellers on the reservation entranced their audience. This was a very different audience, and she knew she must tell different stories to hold their attention. To please her white listeners, she replaced the sounds of wind whispering, meadowlarks singing, and buffalos stampeding with the overblown language of oratory.

She started her speech by reminding everyone of the gentle, generous culture of her people and how badly the *wašíčun* had treated them. She concluded by regurgitating the lessons of boarding school that had been drummed into her: If Indians were to rise from their ignorance, they had to adopt the "white man's ways."

Out of the principles of the Great Charter has arisen in America a nation of free men and free institutions. Among its rivers and mountains, in its stately forests and on its broad prairies, millions of workers have built great factories, commercial highways, fruitful farms, and productive mines. America has great buildings befitting its social progress. And scholars, statesmen, and religious leaders give expression and force to the religious and humanitarian zeal of a great people.

But let us now roll back the tides of time four hundred years to when America was one great wilderness. Over the trees of the forest curls the smoke of the wigwam. The hills resound with the hunter's shout that dies away with the fleeing deer. On the river glides the hunter's canoe. In his wigwam Laughing Water weaves rainbow-tinted beads into his moccasins. In the evening glow the eyes of the children brighten as the aged brave tells his fantastic legends.

The red man lived in reverential awe of the Great Spirit. The Indians heard his voice in the wind. They saw his frown in a cloud and his smile in the sunbeam. Quick to string his bow for vengeance, he was always ready to bury the hatchet or smoke the pipe of peace. Never was he the first to break a treaty or known to betray a friend.

The invasion by a paler race did not dismay the hospitable Indian. Samoset voiced the feeling of his people as he stood among the winter-weary Pilgrims and cried, "Welcome, Englishmen." The Indian did not cling selfishly to his lands. Willingly he divided with Roger Williams and with William Penn. To Jesuit, to Quaker, to all who kept their faith with him, his loyalty never faltered.

Unfortunately civilization is not an unmixed blessing. Vices begin to creep into the Indian's life. He learns to crave the European liquid fire. Broken treaties shake his faith in the newcomers. The white man's bullet decimates his tribes and drives him from his home.

What if he fought? His forests were felled; his game frightened away; his streams of finny shoals usurped. He loved his family and defended them. He loved the land of which he was rightful owner. He loved his fathers' traditions and their graves. Do you wonder that he avenged the loss of his home and being ruthlessly driven from his temples of worship? Is patriotism only in white men's hearts?

The charge of cruelty has been brought against the Indian. But let it be remembered, before condemning the red man, that while he burned and tortured frontiersmen, Puritan Boston burned witches and hanged Quakers, and the Southern aristocrat beat his slaves and set bloodhounds on the track of him who dared aspire to freedom. The Indian brought no greater stain upon his name than these.

Today the Indian is pressed almost to the farther sea. America entered upon her career of freedom and prosperity with the declaration that "all men are born free and equal." Can you as Americans deny equal opportunities to an American people in their struggle to rise from ignorance and degradation?

We come from mountain fastnesses, from cheerless plains, from far-off low-wooded streams, seeking the "white man's ways." We seek labor and honest independence. We seek knowledge and wisdom and your skills in industry and in art. We seek to understand your laws and the genius of your noble institutions. We seek to unite with yours our claim to a common country. We seek to stand side by side with you in ascribing honor to our nation's flag. America, I love thee. "Thy people shall be my people, and thy God my God."

After my concluding words, I heard the same applause given to the other orators. As I walked down the steps of the stage, I was astounded to receive from my fellow students a large bouquet of roses tied with flowing ribbons. With the lovely flowers I fled back to my seat. This friendly token was a rebuke to me for the hard feelings I had borne them.

Later the judges awarded me first place. There was a mad uproar in the hall. My classmates sang and shouted my name at the top of their lungs and the disappointed students howled and brayed into fearfully dissonant tin trumpets. Happy students rushed forward to offer their congratulations. I could not conceal a smile when they wished to escort me in a procession to the students' parlor. Thanking them for their kind spirit, I walked with the night to my little room.

A month later Gertrude was chosen to represent Earlham in a competition of college orators at Indianapolis. She was the only woman speaker and the only Indian. Seated in the large hall, she could not help but be aware of the many pairs of curious eyes staring at her, though she did not allow her face to register any feelings of self-consciousness. She listened to the other contestants, and when some belittled Indians, she did not let her anger show either.

Gertrude was the last speaker. When her name was called, Earlham students cheered and waved canes with streamers. She repeated the speech that had won her first prize the month before. When she finished, her classmates cheered her again, but some students from other colleges humiliated her.

Before that vast ocean of eyes, some college rowdies threw out a large white flag with a drawing of a most forlorn Indian girl on it. Under this they had printed in bold black letters words that ridiculed the college which was represented by a "squaw." Such worse than barbarian rudeness embittered me. While we waited for the verdict of the judges, I gleamed fiercely upon the throng of palefaces. My teeth were hard set, for the white flag still floated insolently in the air.

Anxiously we watched the man carry the envelope with the final decision toward the stage. There were two prizes given that night, and one of them was mine! The evil spirit laughed within me when the white flag dropped out of sight, and the hands which furled it hung limp in defeat.

Leaving the crowd as quickly as possible, I was soon in my room. The rest of the night I sat in an armchair and gazed into the crackling fire. I laughed no more in triumph when alone. The little taste of victory did not satisfy a hunger in my heart. In my mind I saw my mother far away on the Western plains, and she was angry at me.

The telephone brought word of Gertrude's triumph to Earlham students who had not gone to Indianapolis, and they raced through the campus shouting the happy news. Banners and bunting were draped over the entrance of Earlham Hall and wrapped around its staircase and in the student parlor. Miniature American flags were placed in the windows. When Gertrude arrived the next day, the students cheered her at the college entrance. Three days later a reception in her honor was held.

Shortly after her victory, Gertrude fell ill. College officials considered her illness too serious to let her remain on campus and sent her to recuperate with a family in a nearby town. The illness returned the next year, and she was too sick to continue college. No medical records have yet been found to confirm what disease she had, but in a letter to a friend a few years later, Gertrude wrote of a recurrence of malaria. For the rest of her life she had chronic bouts of debilitating flus, lung infections, and stomach disorders.

Becoming a Teacher

When illness left me unable to continue my college course, my pride kept me from returning to my mother. Had she known of my worn condition, she would have said the white man's papers were not worth the freedom and health I had lost by them. Such a rebuke from my mother would have been unbearable, as it was far too true to be comfortable. There was no doubt that the direction in which I wished to spend my energies was in working for the Indian race.

In July 1897, when Gertrude felt sufficiently recovered from malaria, she went to teach at Carlisle, the U.S. Indian Industrial School, which was the most well-known Indian boarding school in the United States. Non-Indians often assumed that it was a college because its football team won many victories against college teams, and its band gave outstanding public concerts. Most students did not graduate from Carlisle, and even fewer went to college, for the curriculum did not prepare them for higher education.

THE FLIGHT OF RED BIRD

I found myself, tired and hot, in a black veil of smoke, standing wearily on a street corner of Carlisle, Pennsylvania, an old-fashioned town, waiting for a car. In a few moments I should be on the school grounds, where a new work was ready for my inexperienced hands.

Upon entering the school campus, I was surprised at the thickly clustered buildings, which made it a quaint little village, much more interesting than the town itself. The large trees among the houses gave the place a cool, refreshing shade, and the grass a deeper green.

I made myself known and was shown to my room—a small carpeted room with ghastly walls and ceiling. The two windows, both on the same side, were curtained with heavy muslin yellowed with age. A bed was in one corner of the room, and opposite it was a square pine table covered with a black woolen blanket.

Without removing my hat, I seated myself in one of the two stiff-backed chairs placed beside the table. For several heart-throbs I sat still, looking from ceiling to floor, from wall to wall, trying hard to imagine years of contentment here. While I was wondering if my exhausted strength would sustain me through this undertaking, I heard a heavy tread stop at my door. Opening it, I met the imposing figure of a stately gray-haired man. With a light straw hat in his left hand, and his right hand extended for greeting, he smiled kindly upon me. For some reason I was awed by his wondrous height and his strong square shoulders, which I felt were a finger's length above my head.

I was always slight, and my serious illness in the early spring had made me look rather frail and languid. His quick eye measured my height and breadth. He looked into my face. I imagined that a visible shadow flitted across his face as he let my hand fall. I knew he was no other than my employer, Captain Richard Henry Pratt.

Richard Henry Pratt, ca. 1900. (Courtesy of the Cumberland County Historical Society, Carlisle, PA.)

"So you are the little Indian girl who created the excitement among the college orators!" he said, more to himself than to me. I thought I heard a subtle note of disappointment in his voice. Looking in from where he stood, with one sweeping glance, he asked if I lacked anything for my room.

THE FLIGHT OF RED BIRD

After he turned to go, I listened to his step until it grew faint and was lost in the distance. I was aware that my car-smoked appearance from the train had not concealed the lines of pain on my face. For a short time my spirit laughed at my ill fortune, and I entertained the idea of exerting myself to make an improvement. But as I tossed my hat off, a leaden weakness came over me, and I felt as if years of weariness lay like water-soaked logs upon me. I threw myself upon the bed and, closing my eyes, forgot my good intention.

A Second Visit Home

After a month of teaching, Gertrude was sent to the Yankton Reservation to recruit students. Now twenty-one years old, she had not been home in six years.

I needed nourishment, but the midsummer's travel across the continent to search the hot prairies for overconfident parents who would entrust their children to strangers was a lean pasture. However, I dwelled on the hope of seeing my mother again.

The intense heat and the sticky car smoke that followed my homeward trail did not noticeably restore my vitality. Hour after hour I gazed from the train window upon the country receding rapidly from me. I noticed the gradual expansion of the horizon as we emerged out of the forests into the plains. The great high buildings, whose towers overlooked the dense woodlands, and whose gigantic clusters formed large cities, diminished, together with the groves, until only little log cabins lay snugly in the bosom of the vast prairie. The cloud shadows which drifted about on the waving yellow of long-dried grasses thrilled me like the meeting of old friends.

THE FLIGHT OF RED BIRD

I left the iron horse at a small railroad station consisting of a single frame house with a rickety boardwalk around it. I was thirty miles from my mother and my brother David. A strong hot wind seemed determined to blow my hat off and return me to olden days when I roamed bareheaded over the prairie.

After my train was gone, I stood on the platform in deep solitude. In the distance I saw the gently rolling land leap up into bare hills. At their bases a broad gray road wound itself round until it came by the station.

Among these hills I rode in a light conveyance, with a trusty driver, whose unkempt flaxen hair hung shaggy about his ears and his leathery neck of reddish tan. From accident or decay he had lost one of his long front teeth. His cheeks were of a brick red. His moist blue eyes, blurred and bloodshot, twitched involuntarily. For a long time he had driven through grass and snow from this solitary station to the reservation. His weather-stained clothes badly fit his warped shoulders. He was stooped, and his protruding chin, with its tuft of dry flax, nodded as monotonously as did the head of his faithful beast.

As we drove I looked about me, recognizing old familiar skylines of rugged bluffs and round-topped hills. By the roadside I caught glimpses of various plants whose sweet roots were delicacies among my people. When I saw the first cone-shaped wigwam, I could not help uttering an exclamation, which caused my driver a sudden jump out of his drowsy nodding.

At the eastern edge of the reservation I grew very impatient and restless. I wondered what my mother would say upon seeing her little daughter grown tall. I had not written her the day of my arrival, thinking I would surprise her. Crossing a ravine thicketed with low shrubs and plum bushes, we approached an acre of wild sunflowers. Just beyond this nature's garden was my mother's log cabin. Close by stood a canvas-covered wigwam. The driver pulled his horses to a stop, and my mother appeared.

I had expected her to run out to greet me, but she stood still, staring at the weather-beaten man at my side. At length, when her loftiness became unbearable, I called to her, "Mother, why do you stop?"

This seemed to break the evil moment, and she hastened out to hold my head against her cheek.

"My daughter, what madness possessed you to bring home such a fellow?" she asked, pointing at the driver, who was fumbling in his pockets for change while he held the bill I gave him between his jagged teeth.

"Bring him! Why, no, Mother, he has brought me. He is a driver!" I exclaimed.

Upon this revelation, my mother threw her arms about me and apologized for her mistaken inference. We laughed away the momentary hurt. Then she built a brisk fire on the ground in the tipi. She hung a blackened coffeepot on one of the prongs of a forked pole which leaned over the flames. Placing a pan on a heap of red embers, she baked some unleavened bread. This light lunch she brought into the cabin and arranged on a table covered with a checkered oilcloth.

My mother had never gone to school, and though she meant always to give up her own customs for such of the white man's ways as pleased her, she made only compromises. Her two windows were curtained with a pink-flowered print. The logs of the cabin were unstained, and rudely carved with the axe so as to fit into one another. The sod roof was trying to boast of tiny sunflowers, the seeds of which had probably been planted by the constant wind. As I leaned my head against the logs, I smelled the peculiar odor that I could never forget. The rains had soaked the earth and roof so that the smell of damp clay was but the natural breath of the dwelling.

"Mother, why isn't your house cemented? Do you have no interest in a more comfortable shelter?" I asked.

"My child, I am old and do not work with beads anymore." My mother was then about sixty-two years old. "And your brother has lost his job and we are left without means to buy even a morsel of food."

When I last heard from David he was an issue clerk for the Bureau of Indian Affairs on the reservation. I was surprised to learn that he no longer had this job. Seeing the puzzled expression on my face, my mother continued, "Oh, has David not told you that the Great Father at Washington sent a white son to take your brother's pen from him? Since then he has not been able to make use of his education."

I found no words with which to answer satisfactorily. I found no reason with which to cool my inflamed feelings. David was a whole day's journey off on the prairie, and my mother did not expect him until the next day. We were silent.

When, at length, I raised my head to hear more clearly the moaning of the wind in the corner logs, I noticed the daylight streaming into the dingy room through several places where the logs fitted unevenly. I urged my mother to tell me more about David's trouble.

But she only said, "This village has been these many winters a refuge for white robbers. The Indian cannot complain to the Great Father in Washington without suffering for it. David tried to secure justice for our tribe in a small matter, and you see the folly of it."

Again, though she stopped to hear what I might say, I was silent.

"My child, there is only one source of justice. I have been praying steadfastly to the Great Spirit to avenge our wrongs," she said, seeing I did not move my lips.

"Mother, don't pray again! The Great Spirit does not care if we live or die. Let us not look for good or justice; then we shall not be disappointed."

"My child, do not talk so madly." She stroked my head as she used to do when I was a small child.

One evening Mother and I sat in the dim starlight. We were facing the river as we talked about the shrinking limits of the village. She told me about the white squatters who had rushed to make claims on the land and now lived in caves dug in the long ravines of the high hills across the river. As she was telling this, I spied a small glimmering light in the bluffs.

"That is a white man's lodge, where you see the burning fire," she said. A short distance from it, only a little lower than the first, was another light. As I became accustomed to the night, I saw more and more twinkling lights scattered all along the wide black margin of the river.

My mother looked toward the distant firelight and chanted the same litany against the cruel paleface as she had in my childhood: "My daughter, beware of the paleface. It was the cruel paleface who caused the death of your sister and your uncle. He is the hypocrite who reads with one eye, 'Thou shalt not kill,' and with the other eye gloats upon the sufferings of the Indian race." She sprang to her feet and held her outstretched fingers toward the settlers' lodges, as if an invisible power passed from her fingers to the evil at which she aimed.

Gertrude was surprised by the lights across the river, for they had not been there six years before. Over the summer she learned how white settlers had come to live on the reservation.

Ten years earlier, as part of their policy to force Indians to give up tribal life, Congress had passed the Dawes Act, which redistributed reservation land. Once, the tribe owned all land communally. Now, each "competent" head of a family received 160 acres (a quarter of a square mile). Eighty additional acres went to each family member over eighteen; younger children received forty acres. This land was put in trust for the Indians, not to be sold for twenty-five years.

Most tribal leaders had protested the law because it weakened the unity of the tribe: Now people had to deal with the federal government as individuals, not as a nation. On five separate occasions, followers of Yankton headman Feathers Around His Neck prevented government surveyors from setting foot on the reservation. Only when soldiers from a nearby fort arrived with rifles did his followers stop their resistance.

The surveying was completed. Then the Indian agent and the missionaries began determining who was "competent" enough to own land. "Competent" really meant those Indians who accepted white culture—those who did not wear traditional dress, who spoke English, and who attended church regularly.

Under the new law whatever land was not given out could be sold to non-Indians. The tribe still owned 167,000 acres communally from the 430,000 acres reserved for them in the 1858 treaty. The federal government wanted those acres for white settlers but by law needed the tribe's approval to get them. When Yankton leaders protested, the Bureau agent plotted to get around their disapproval. He put tribal members who supported selling the land on a new council that replaced the headmen as the tribe's representatives and gave the new group the power to approve all federal proposals. One Yankton man was promised a government post if he gathered enough signatures supporting the sale. The plot worked: All the communal land was sold to white settlers. As a result of the Dawes Act, 138 million acres of Indian-owned lands in the United States were reduced to 47 million acres.

When Gertrude's brother David lost his government job, he began farming so he could feed his wife and two small children. Other Yankton men, threatened by the agent with losing their family's food rations if they did not farm, picked up plows too. In their haste the surveyors had marked off much land that was unsuitable for agriculture, and many Yankton men found that nothing would grow on their allotments. David was luckier than most. His soil yielded plentiful harvests.

Most Yanktons were desperately poor and dependent on federal food and goods. Fraud, bad harvests, and unemployment had forced them to sell more than half their land. Gertrude's kinfolk lived too far away from each other to hold the storytelling evenings of her childhood. It was hard enough to get together for special events. The tribe's unity had been destroyed.

Realizations

In the fall of 1897 Gertrude returned to teach at Carlisle. A few blocks away Thomas Marshall, a Lakota from the Pine Ridge Reservation, was enrolled as a sophomore at Dickinson College. Gertrude and Thomas had been classmates at White's. The details of their romance are not known, but they became engaged at some point during the eighteen months that Gertrude was at Carlisle.

Gertrude's teaching responsibilities kept her busy, but she still found time to study the violin again and appeared as a soloist with Carlisle's orchestra at public concerts. The New York *Musical Courier* described her as "charmingly artistic and graceful"; the *Brooklyn Times* called her a "picture to be remembered." She was discovered and embraced by the white world.

In August 1898 Gertrude Käsebier, a well-known photographer, invited her to New York City to spend part of her vacation. Käsebier photographed her then. The portrait is typical of hundreds taken at that time of "genteel" white women.

Gertrude wears a long white dress with puffy sleeves and a high-gathered waist, a dress that Shakespeare's Juliet might have worn. Her black hair rests on her shoulders. Her hands

Zitkala-Ša, August 1898. (Courtesy of the National Anthropological Archives, Smithsonian Institution.)

sit gracefully on an open book on her lap. Her eyes look wistfully at the camera. Delicate flowered wallpaper completes the setting for this idealized image of young womanhood.

Despite all this attention and her love for Thomas, Gertrude was increasingly unhappy, for she was beginning to realize the price she had paid for "becoming white."

As months passed at Carlisle, I slowly comprehended that the large army of white teachers in Indian schools had a larger missionary creed than I had expected. It was one which included self-preservation quite as much as Indian education. I burned with indignation upon discovering on every side shameful instances. Even the rare ones who worked nobly for my race were powerless to choose workmen like themseves. To be sure, a man was sent from the Great Father to inspect Indian schools, but what he saw was usually the students' sample work *made* for exhibition. I was nettled by the sly cunning of those who hoodwinked the Indian's pale Father at Washington.

My illness, which prevented the conclusion of my college course, together with my mother's stories of the encroaching settlers, left me in no mood to strain my eyes in searching for latent good in my coworkers. At this stage of my own evolution I was ready to curse men of small capacity for being the dwarfs their God had made them. In the process of my education I had lost all consciousness of the nature world about me. So when a hidden rage took me to the small white-walled prison which I then called my room, I unknowingly turned away from my own salvation. Alone in my room I sat like the petrified Indian woman of whom my mother used to tell me. I wished my heart's burdens would turn me to unfeeling stone.

For the white man's papers I had given up my faith in the Great Spirit. For these papers I had forgotten the healing in trees and brooks. On account of my mother's simple view of life, and my lack of any, I gave her up also. I made no friends among the race of people I loathed. Like a slender tree, I had been uprooted from my mother, nature, and the Great Spirit. I was shorn of my branches, which had waved in sympathy and love for home and friends. The natural coat of bark which had protected my over-sensitive nature was scraped off to the very quick. Now I seemed to be a cold bare pole, planted in a strange earth.

One weary day in the schoolroom, a new idea presented itself to me. It was a new way of solving the problem of my inner self. I liked it.

In January 1899 Gertrude resigned as a teacher to go to Boston to study music at the New England Conservatory of Music. A Quaker woman from Indiana had offered to support her. Though engaged to Thomas, she would not let that love stop her from studying music, even if it meant being separated from him.

Boston was alive with concerts and stimulating lectures where people discussed the latest books and politics. Her teachers were encouraging though demanding. She began to distinguish between non-Indians who viewed her as "the accomplished savage" and those who were genuinely interested in her. For the first time in her life she felt comfortable among whites and at school made two lifelong friends, Gracie and Ethel. In her new environment she reflected on the idea of the boarding schools and decided they were a cruel educational experiment.

In Boston I remembered how, from morning till evening, many specimens of civilized peoples visited the Indian school. The city folks with canes and eyeglasses, the countrymen with sunburned cheeks and clumsy feet, forgot their relative social ranks in an ignorant curiosity about the Indian students. These Christians were astounded at seeing the children of people they believed were savage warriors so docile and industrious.

As answers to their shallow inquiries they received the students' sample work to look upon. Examining the neatly figured pages and gazing upon the Indian girls and boys bending over their books, the white visitors walked out of the schoolhouse well satisfied that they were educating the children of the red man.

Many passed idly through the Indian schools, afterward to boast of their charity to the North American Indian. But few paused to question whether real life or long-lasting death lies beneath this semblance of civilization.

The "Indian" in Gertrude had reemerged, and with it anger and excruciating pain over what she had lost by being forced "to become white." She cringed at the term "primitive" to describe Native Americans. Indian culture was not inferior to white culture; in many ways she believed it was superior.

THE FLIGHT OF RED BIRD

Four months after Gertrude went to Boston, Thomas unexpectedly died of measles. Soon after, her Quaker sponsor wrote her that she could no longer give her money. In despair, Gertrude turned to her new friend Ethel for comfort. Ethel told her to pray to the Great Spirit to guide her; the idea of writing about her life emerged from her prayers.

Gertrude knew her life story mirrored what had happened to thousands of other Indians forced to renounce their culture. Gone were the days of armed struggle between Indians and whites. The lecture platform and pen were the new weapons. She would use the language that had been forced upon her to attack the very institutions that had imposed it. She took her fury and harnessed it into dramatizing the plight of Native Americans. Her life story flowed out of her. The magazine *Atlantic Monthly* published her reminiscences in three installments—January, February, and March 1900. She signed the articles with the name Zitkala-Ša.

Like many Indians, Yanktons were given several names over a lifetime. At birth children were named according to their position in the family (first born, second born) or their sex (*win* at the end of a name indicated a girl). Later, a medicine person bestowed an honor name representing a great deed of an ancestor. There were nicknames, and deed names given when someone performed an unusually brave act. Gertrude's mother had never given her an Indian name.

Gertrude felt estranged from her family and didn't want to use the last name Simmons. More important, she wanted to be identified as an Indian. She named herself Zitkala-Ša. *Zitkala* means bird, *ša* means red.

Zitkala-Ša never explained her choice of this pseudonym or why she did not put *win* at the end of the name to identify herself as a woman. But she chose a fitting name: This red bird had been plucked as a fledgling from her nest on the reservation and caged in a boarding school. It had taken fourteen years for her damaged wings to heal enough so that she could fly. Now she felt strong enough to redefine the path of her life and to reclaim her Indian identity.

The critics praised her writing and honesty, but Richard Henry Pratt denounced her for "not once" writing about "the happier side of her school days or even hinting at the many friends who did so much to lead her from poverty and insignificance into the full and rich existence that she enjoys today."

Zitkala-Ša defended herself in a letter to Carlisle's school newspaper:

> To stir up views and earnest comparisons of theories is one of the ways to benefit my people. No one can dispute my own impressions and bitterness.

Love

Zitkala-Ša looked through the window at the snowflaked sky. It was January 1901, the beginning of her third year in Boston. She felt weary and achy on this snowy night. Maybe it was another attack of malaria, like last summer's. Maybe she should rest and watch the falling flakes, but she had so much to do. She had harmony exercises to complete for tomorrow's class and galley proofs to correct from her children's book, *Old Indian Legends*, and finishing touches on another short story she hoped to sell. No, all that could wait. She would write to Carlos. She had not yet answered his last three letters.

Carlos Montezuma was a doctor of Yavapai descent ten years her senior. At four years old he had been captured by the Pimas in a massacre of his people and sold for thirty dollars to an Italian immigrant, Carlos Gentile. He never saw his family again. Gentile gave his adopted son his own first name and for some reason the name of Montezuma—the last Aztec chieftain, who ruled in the early sixteenth century—for a surname. Gentile brought up his son until business reverses led him to choose William H. Steadman, a Baptist minister, as Carlos's guardian.

Steadman recognized Carlos's exceptional abilities and encouraged him as he worked his way through college and medical school. So did Richard Henry Pratt, who always referred to Carlos in his speeches as an example of what Indians could achieve with education. Now Carlos was practicing medicine in Chicago. He was having a difficult time, for most whites didn't want to go to an Indian doctor.

Carlos Montezuma, 1903. (Courtesy of the Department of Archives and Manuscripts, Arizona State University, Tempe.)

Carlos was smart and handsome and determined to marry Zitkala-Ša. It was almost two years since Thomas had died, but she insisted that love was not possible. Carlos courted her with letters and chocolates. His letters made her happy. She wanted to get to know him better. She wanted him to know her better, to understand the pulls in her life: She needed and loved what she called "artificial" things like classical music, books, and city life, but she also felt a deep admiration for and responsibility to her mother and her kin.

She picked up her pen to write him.

Boston, February 20, 1901

Dear friend,

As for my plans, while the old people last I want to get from them their treasured ideas of life. This I can do by living among them. I mean to "divide my time" between teaching and getting story material. I don't exactly agree with Captain Pratt about the great superiority of non-reservation schools. The <u>old folks</u> have a claim upon us. It is selfish and cruel to abandon them entirely.

You are kind to express a willingness to do anything in your power for me. I know you wish only the best for me. Good will is the most I can accept now, so let me thank you. Let me wish the day's sunshine may enter your soul.

I am your friend,
Zitkala-Ša

She sent Carlos copies of her new stories and he encouraged her to keep writing. Slowly her heart opened to him, but her moods changed frequently. The years at boarding school had left her with "hidden rage" that constantly erupted. In one letter she was cruel; in the next letter, loving.

Early April 1901

Dear friend,

You hope vain things of God for He left love out of my heart in the first place. He <u>cannot</u> bring us together with love when it is the one minus quantity in me. I guess it seems odd to you to find another as stiff-necked in old opinions as your willful self? I have no desire to make definite plans for my future life. I am too independent. I would not like to have to obey another—never!

Good night,
Zitkala

April 12, 1901

My best-est dear,

Sweetheart, this evening I found the first wild rose I have seen this year. I brought it home thinking to send it to you, but it is so withered. I must wait till I can press another in proper time. I wish you were here or I there with you this evening.

I may not feel equal to staying with my mother in Yankton until November. In that case, dear, I would come to you in Chicago. Would that be all right?

Now, I must say "Good night." Happy Dreams to
you. May the Great Spirit guard you for me, my well-
chosen one.

Yours,

Zitkala-Ša

When two of her short stories were published in *Harper's*
magazine, Pratt denounced her again in Carlisle's newspaper
for her negative portrayals of missionaries and educators in
these stories. Zitkala-Ša despised Pratt for his contempt of
Indian culture, but his attack wounded her.

April 13, 1901

Dear friend,

Though I wrote you only last night, I am writing
again because I feel sick. Captain Pratt is pigheaded.
I must live my life. I must think in my own way (since
I cannot help it). I must write the lessons I see. I have
a place in the Universe, and no one can cheat or
crowd me by a single hair's breadth. Just the same I
feel sick way in my heart.

You are not ignorant of the fact that I have many
admirers, but somehow I turn to you for a word of
courage. Shall I continue in my work or shall I keep
still? I will recover from this nausea caused by the
crude morality of those who would be critics of my

art. But I am ill this moment. Ah, I rise. I lift my head!
I laugh at the babble! I guess I am not so sick after all.

Good-by,

Zitkala

Zitkala-Ša planned to spend a year with her mother and asked Carlos to prove his love by coming with her.

April 19, 1901

Dear friend,

You ask why I am going to my mother? I am going to her because she cannot come to me. Visit her only? That is cruel and heartless. I must live with her and show her each day a practical demonstration of my love for her. She will never realize what cost it may mean to me who has acquired so many artificial tastes that they have become my second nature. On the reservation I can write stories and have them published in the East for the so-called civilized peoples.

You ask me if you could make me happy. I don't know. I imagine you might be able to make me happy. You say you love me, but I am no judge. Others say that to me. How am I to know which one is true, for surely all cannot love me alike.

To tell you the honest truth, I am a delusion and a snare. You should love one more able to give you as much and as largely as you give of your heart.

If you agree with me that life is lived most when we love and make individuals happy, you would have to come to me in Yankton. You could do a vast deal of good as agency physician there. But remember I do not ask you to do it. You must do it from choice. If you cannot do it, then you don't love me enough after all. I would forgive you though and keep your friendship sacred in my heart.

I have said enough. I stop until I have your reply. Then I shall be better able to say whether you shall be permitted to meet me in Chicago on my way to the reservation or whether it would be wiser to pass through without your knowledge. I am quite equal for either.

Very sincerely,
Zitkala

Her ultimatum for Carlos to come to Yankton was unrealistic, for she knew he had worked as a doctor on three reservations and had been horrified by conditions. Reservation life was a strange, isolating world to one who knew only white society. Carlos believed Indians had to give up traditional ways to be successful. Zitkala-Ša believed these ways offered a strength and dignity that should not be dismissed in the name of progress. She kept pressing him to come to Yankton and taunted him about other suitors.

◆ ◆ *Love* ◆ ◆

May 1901

Dear friend,

Perhaps the Indians are not human enough to waste your skill upon. Stay in Chicago. I consider my plan a more direct path to my high ideals. It will be a test of my character. I am satisfied that you do not love me enough. I shall never tell you in so many words whether I love you or not. If my giving you the preference to a long list of applicants conveys no meaning to you, words would be sounding metals only. On my list are these men:

1– a well-known German violinist

2– a Harvard professor

3– a Harvard postgraduate

4– a well-known writer

5– a man of a prominent New York family

6– four Western men scattered from Montana to Dakota

I have not counted any of last year's nor those previous, for it would be too long a task. I write all this to show you there are other men who can give me as much as you could. I do not care about a doctor's profession more than those of the others.

So my friend, I cannot stop in your beloved chosen city. I shall pass through because I have to.

Good-by,

Zitkala

The responsibilities of the traditional wife frightened and baffled her. She knew little of cooking, sewing, and housekeeping. And the beadwork that her mother had taught her, that she loved so much, would be of little use in her home with Carlos. Marriage would mean losing her independence. She would become "Mrs. Carlos Montezuma," and the identity for which she had sacrificed so much would be submerged.

May 7, 1901

Dear friend,

Did I not tell you to beware of me? I say I am a delusion and a snare. Do not be too sure of me, for I am the uncertain quantity. I swear I am not yours! I do not belong to anybody. Do not wish to be! First, I like roaming about too well to settle down anywhere. Second, I know absolutely nothing about housekeeping. I would be restless and a burden.

I can help you most as a friend, but never otherwise. Oh, well, we will talk to better advantage in a few days. Now my friend, do be careful. I must warn you again. I am uncertain! Hoping to see you Thursday,

Good-by,

Zitkala

Zitkala-Ša met Carlos in Chicago on her way to Yankton.

May 13, 1901

Dear Carlos,

Oh, you do not know how it affected me to find you had not used my money for my ticket. I felt like burying my face in both my hands and weeping. It was hard to accept it, even from you.

Last night I placed my beautiful red rose on part of my pillow. This morning I awoke but my rose would not be aroused. You were and are so wondrously kind to me. I know it and appreciate it too. How comes it to pass, I wonder. So long I've wandered hither and thither—careless of others as they were of me.

I was very much interested in what you said yesterday about an organization of Indians. Let us not think of asking money of any white man. Let us have nothing to do with Charity from others.

Did you know last evening I didn't want to leave you?

With my best love, Good-by

She agreed that in November they could marry, but she continued to taunt him.

May 28, 1901

My dear friend,

I had a letter from my old mother and she has affected my whole thought again. At least one year I must _give_ her! If you do not wish to wait for me a year, marry when and whom you choose! I must do what seems to me my first duty. I feel that I must be saying some hard things but I cannot pad them with feathers. Perhaps such a revelation would show you how unworthy I am of your devotion.

In an indirect way it may be a kindness to you. I cannot help being _myself._ I think I should indeed feel badly to lose you as my friend, but I am not capable of any effort to be agreeable. Forgive me. I pray you.

Here is a pansy I've had in my room!

Sincerely from one who does not know her own mind.

Zitkala

Two days later she felt only love.

May 30, 1901

My dear Carlos,

I know you _can_ make me happy and I hope I may at _least_ gladden your heart a few days out of a year. I know so little about keeping a house in running order that the undertaking is perfectly appalling to me. And from sheer cowardice I almost back out of the experiment.

I wish I were with you this evening. May I grow more worthy of you, my highly esteemed.

Zitkala

Tormented by how much she had moved away from her people's ways, she feared that life with Carlos in the Red Apple Country might lead her even farther away. His mind excited her and so did his love, but their courtship was terribly foreign to what her mother had taught her. She picked flowers for him. Her people did not use flowers as decoration or love mementos, for they valued a flower's right to exist. Carlos sent her a ring. The ring pleased her, but she did not wear it.

June 1, 1901

My own beloved,

You are right in believing I do not like display. It is my wish to have our wedding informal and very quiet. I am telling my mother—but no one else.

I have not a single picture of you. I wish I had one!

Soon I shall begin to make the beaded cushion covers I promised you. It will be my pleasure. Dear, I want you to be happy, and if it lies in my power, I would like you always to have reason to be proud of your wife "to be" as she is already of you.

Yesterday I received a letter from my publisher asking me to write <u>another</u> volume of stories! I shall gather all I can and do the writing when I am in our home. Sweetheart, would it not be a great work to write many volumes of Indian legends!

Do you remember this rose? It was yours dear and I've kept it a long time. Now I send it to you.

Affectionately,
Zitkala

THE FLIGHT OF RED BIRD

Late June 1901

My dear Montezuma,

You please me by saying there would be a piano in the house. But what do you mean about a brief court-ship? Do you suppose it was evident when I said I would give you the preference? That is annoying to say the least. I've a big mind to marry the other fellow and let you find elsewhere the properly prolonged courtship! I set aside the stated month November. Hereafter that time will be indefinite.

Zitkala

The "other fellow" was Raymond Telephause Bonnin, a Yankton from her reservation. Raymond's father, Joseph, was of French descent and his mother, Emily, a Yankton. From his maternal grandmother Raymond had learned the traditional stories and ceremonies and proud history of his great-grandfather Hejata, once head of the Ikmú (Wild Cat) clan.

Raymond was twenty-two and Zitkala-Ša was twenty-six. Raymond took her horseback riding, and the rolling hills and open prairie filled both their hearts with joy. He shared his dreams and disappointments. He had returned from boarding school determined to farm, but after three unsuccessful harvests he knew that his allotment, like so many on the reservation, was unsuitable. Now he worked for the Indian Service helping their people. Zitkala-Ša shared her dual dream of capturing traditional stories on paper and studying music.

Being with Raymond reconnected her to her people, language, and traditional ways. She repaired her relationship with her brother David and his wife, Victoria.

August 11, 1901

Dear Montezuma,

Please don't get cross with me, for then you will lose control of me entirely. I have had a difficult summer with a cranky old woman by the merest accident my mother. I have just exactly <u>all</u> I can bear. I have felt pretty nigh desperate more times than my pride would permit my telling. This very night that I write I have been needlessly tortured by Mother's crazy tongue till all hell seems set loose upon my heels. And I feel wicked enough to kill her on the spot or else run wild.

Where I am to go or when and what I am to do, no one knows.

Z

Raymond was there to offer sympathy and understanding. He called her Sky Star and gave her a ruby ring as a token of his esteem. She wore his ring, not Carlos's. The friendship grew into love. She broke off her engagement to Carlos and sent back his ring.

August 15, 1901

My friend,

> *As for our former relation, I have nothing more to say. It is gone. But I will be as good a friend as I can if you will permit me to be. If not, then this is the last letter.*

> > *Good-by,*
> > > *Zitkala*

Six days later she decided to give Carlos "another chance." She asked him to send the ring back. The rift between them continued through the mail, sharply contrasting with her easy and fulfilling relationship with Raymond.

August 31, 1901

Dear Montezuma,

> *You should have given me up and thanked your lucky stars for a narrow escape. If we marry, it will be when you have carried out my wish to come to Yankton and work here, not before. I simply cannot leave my mother out of my plans without feeling like a criminal. If you cannot comply, we will postpone the day while I teach here and take care of my mother.*

> > *Good-by,*
> > > *Zitkala*

Two months later she chose between the two men.

October 19, 1901

Dear friend,

I do not come to you this month nor any other for the simple reason of our nonconjugal temperaments. I have a friend out here who claims all I can give by the laws of natural affinity. In a few days I shall return your ring to you. There, I have written plainly because you have made me cross. I can always respect you as a friend but never more.

Let me wish you success in your chosen world and work. Mine lie in places "barren and foreign" to your acquired taste.

Good-by,

Z

Zitkala-Ša felt that she belonged within the Indian community and knew she could not live there with Carlos. On August 10, 1902, Zitkala-Ša and Raymond were married.

In December Raymond was offered a job with the Indian Service on the Uintah Reservation in Utah. He wanted the job but didn't have enough money for travel expenses. His brother, Henry, gave him four hundred dollars and told him to pay it back when he could. Raymond and Zitkala-Ša headed West.

The Uintah Reservation
1903–1916

Mr. and Mrs. Raymond Bonnin

Zitkala-Ša watched the Ute children line up on the wooden walk that led from the Uintah boarding school to their dormitories. The six- and seven-year-old girls, with clipped hair falling into their faces, stood straight and stiff in their drab

Ute girls at Whiterocks Boarding School, Uintah Reservation, late 1930s. (Courtesy of the Uintah County Library Regional History Center, Uintah County Public Library, L. C. Thorne Collection.)

uniforms. The boys, in dark suits, with caps covering their shorn hair, looked equally ill at ease. No one seeing these well-scrubbed faces and neatly dressed children would ever guess how many suffered from chronic tuberculosis and body and head lice.

Ute boys at Whiterocks Boarding School, Uintah Reservation, late 1930s. (Courtesy of the Uintah County Library Regional History Center, Uintah County Public Library, L. C. Thorne Collection.)

Three years ago, in 1903, when she and Raymond had arrived on the reservation, she had visited the boarding school. The pain of her own childhood flared up when she saw the loneliness and confusion in the children's eyes. She felt the white teachers would never comprehend their isolation or the damage being inflicted on them by this education. She wanted to help make their lives better than hers had been at boarding school. She wrote to the Indian Bureau asking for a teaching job. No one responded to her request. She wrote again. And again—until finally she was hired on a temporary basis. She was lucky to get even that, for there was no other employment on the reservation.

The matron signaled the children, and they walked slowly to their dreary dormitories with splintered floors and cracked walls and windows. The autumn nights were still warm, but in winter no amount of wood or coal could warm the girls' dormitory with its paper roof. And if one night a kerosene lamp accidently tipped over, the roof would burst into flames in minutes, and the children would never get down the narrow, rickety staircase to safety in time.

The school superintendent had sent many requests to Washington for money to repair the dormitory and to install electric lights, but his requests had been ignored. They would continue to be ignored. There was nothing she could do to change that.

She mounted her horse and headed home. After three years in Utah, her eyes still could not adjust to the vastness of the landscape. Wherever she looked was endless sky interrupted only slightly by clumps of sagebrush and clusters of cottonwood trees and cedars. The Uintah Reservation was now 284,000 acres of horizon hemmed in by mountain ranges, vertical craters of red on three sides. The rust earth of this dry desert country in northeastern Utah was stunning, but very different from the green rolling hills of South Dakota and the long stretch of the Missouri River visible from her mother's cabin.

A mile from home Zitkala-Ša was no longer the only person on the road. It was issue day. The Utes were returning home after a day at the Indian agency at Fort Duchesne, the army base on the reservation. For hours they had stood in the sun, waiting for the Indian agents to divide up the dry foods, slaughter the cattle, and distribute the meat. The Ute men

Issue day, Uintah Reservation, ca. 1905. (Courtesy of the Photographic Archives, Harold B. Lee Library, Brigham Young University, Provo, UT.)

wore loose cotton shirts and trousers; the women, baggy cotton dresses tied at the waist with nondescript strips of cloth or rope. They had bought the cloth from the Indian trader at double and triple its worth. Stacked on their wagons and on the backs of the horses were their meager rations.

Twenty-five years before, when the Utes had lived in Colorado, their diet of fruits, nuts, roots, buffalo, and deer had been rich in vitamins and minerals. But here wild game was scarce. The Utes had not been allowed to bring their livestock to the reservation, and they were not allowed to leave here, even to hunt. They were now as dependent on government rations of fatty meat, flour, coffee, and sugar as the Yanktons were in South Dakota. Malnutrition was one of the many diseases that had befallen this once-independent people.

The road got more cluttered as Zitkala-Ša neared home. The Bonnins' small cottage was in a cluster of buildings at Fort Duchesne. Home was cramped with four adults and their three-year-old son, Ohiya. Raymond's father had come for one of his extended visits of three months or so. Most of the year he lived with Raymond's brother, Henry, and his family. The fourth adult in their home was an eighty-three-year-old Oglala Sioux named Bad Hand. When Raymond had learned that Bad Hand was living in a hut in the mountains, barely subsisting on small wild game and roots, he had brought him to live with them.

A meeting of tribal leaders from the three Ute bands was in progress under the cottonwood tree in the Bonnins' front yard. In the past three years the Utes had come to depend on Raymond. He was one of five Bureau clerks who supervised the buying of goods. He personally inspected wagons, horses, lumber, bricks, cement, lime, hammers, even nails. He examined meat and flour to assure its freshness and tallied the bills. Too often he thought the charges were excessive and called in the white suppliers. They resented being questioned by an Indian, but Raymond didn't care, nor did he back down.

Word spread that Raymond was incorruptible, and Ute tribal leaders began bringing him their problems. Raymond's supervisor was not pleased by his pointing out overcharges by white contractors, nor was he pleased with the frequent tribal councils held in Raymond's yard.

Raymond was balancing Ohiya on one knee and taking notes on the other knee. Zitkala-Ša tied her horse to the fence, and despite her weariness after a day of teaching, she relieved Raymond of Ohiya and of note taking.

The subject, as always, was land and money. The Utes still owned 7 million acres in Colorado. Coal had been found on 700,000 of those acres, and they were determined to be compensated for it. Raymond offered to write a law firm in the East to look into the matter.

There were also problems regarding reservation land. As in South Dakota, white settlers were clamoring for land here in Utah. Utah's Mormons had previously rejected this part of the state as too barren, but now they wanted it. Three years before, a federal official had sat under this same cottonwood tree and tried to "convince" the Utes to take their allotments, so the federal government could legally sell to white settlers whatever land was not given out. The Utes were outraged and protested this violation of the treaty they had signed in good faith. The federal official told them emphatically that the reservation land would be sold to outsiders with or without their permission.

A delegation of the "unconvinced" went to Washington to protest in person to "the Great White Father," President Theodore Roosevelt, but his ears were closed to their pleas. The federal government took away over 2 million acres. One million was added to a forest reserve, the other million set aside for white homesteaders. Now more Mormons lived on the reservation than Utes.

Finally accepting that they were beaten, most Utes took their allotments and found out that the best agricultural land had been reserved for Mormon settlers. Four hundred Utes had packed up and gone to the Pine Ridge Reservation in South Dakota. They were still there, resisting all efforts to be returned.

That evening Raymond reread old treaties, hoping to find legal proof of these injustices in the tangle of federal regulations and agreements. He drafted a letter asking a law firm in Washington, D.C., to take the land-claim case. Zitkala-Ša typed up the meeting notes and then a portion of the family histories she was compiling on each Ute family. Raymond was convinced this information would be invaluable when they went to court to get monetary compensation for land.

Zitkala-Ša was happy in Utah. She and Raymond were needed here. Despite not having a law degree, Raymond Bonnin acted as the Utes' lawyer, and Mrs. Raymond Bonnin, or Gertie, as she was affectionately called, was their private secretary. It was unstated but agreed. She liked being called Mrs. Bonnin. She had chosen the right man for a lifemate and was proud to take his name. Three years later, in 1909, Zitkala-Ša felt quite different about life on the reservation.

On a night like so many others, the children were enrapt listening to Bad Hand's stories of the great battles when the Sioux had triumphed over the *wasicun*. David's daughter Irene had come to stay with them a year ago, and she loved Bad Hand's stories as much as her younger cousin did. Later Zitkala-Ša would tell an Iktomi story. Then the children would play piano duets. Her pupils were exceptionally musical and needed little coaxing to perform.

Evenings like this rekindled warm memories of the *tiyóspaye*, but hearing her language and the old stories did not blunt the persistent ache in her heart. She felt trapped and isolated here. She needed to be with people who cared about music and books and ideas. Hardly anyone on the reservation understood her love of "artificial" things. Why had she agreed to come to such a barren place, so far from civilization, to be surrounded by such coarseness and greed?

The soldiers at Fort Duchesne spent most of their time drinking and gambling in the saloon or visiting the house of prostitution. The never-ending corruption at the Indian Bureau sickened her. The acting Indian agent disliked Raymond and was always looking for an opportunity to criticize him. The Utes had finally won a judgment of $3 million for their Colorado land but had seen none of it. The Bureau superintendent controlled it and rumors were flying that he intended to use it to build roads. But where? And why? There were already more than enough roads on the reservation.

There was no justice for Indians. The Utes barely had enough to eat while white speculators reaped huge profits buying and selling Indian allotments. Powerless and hopeless, many Utes, even small children, had turned to alcohol and gambling.

And what about her dreams of writing? Her publisher in Boston wanted a second collection of traditional stories. Stored away in a box were her typed notes from the storytelling sessions of the Yankton elders. Given some quiet time, she would shape and reshape her sentences until her written words captured their poetry. She was away from the fort now, but she had no quiet time.

She and Raymond had bought land intending to start a horse ranch, but she soon realized she didn't want to be a rancher. Pitching hay and mucking out stalls was drudgery, like farming. Luckily Raymond agreed with her. Since land was the most valuable commodity on the reservation, they decided not to sell theirs, but to rent it. She was at the ranch supervising the building of two barns and an irrigation system. When these improvements were finished, they would lease their land to one of many Mormons wanting more acreage.

Their ranch was too far away from Raymond's office for him to return home each day after work, so he was living in the cottage at Fort Duchesne while she stayed at the ranch.

She was lonely without him, but the work had to be done. They needed money.

Her temporary teaching job had ended. Small as her salary had been, it was sorely missed. Now they had nothing extra to repay Raymond's brother, Henry, or to help her seventy-four-year-old mother, who was barely scraping by. At the end of this month their $550 bank loan was due. Where would they get the money? She had tried to sell part of her allotment at Yankton, but so far there were no buyers.

She picked up Father Martin's photograph from her desk. When she felt lonely or discouraged, she often looked at it. She would write to ask him to pray for her. Perhaps his prayers would bring the much-needed money.

Father Martin was a Benedictine priest from the Standing Rock Reservation in South Dakota. The Bonnins had spent last winter there, and her long-standing antagonism against missionaries had evaporated when she had observed the goodness of the Benedictine fathers and brothers there. Their commitment and love for the people had so affected her that she had converted to Catholicism. At birth Raymond had been baptized a Catholic, but he had not attended church in years. However, when she converted, Sundays found him with her at mass in South Dakota.

There was no Catholic church or even a priest here. Most of the white Bureau employees were Episcopalians, and many were prejudiced against Catholics. Most of the white settlers were Mormons. She missed being among Catholics. She missed the comfort and ritual of the Sunday service. She would ask Father Martin to write the bishop of Utah and have him assign a priest here, to help her, to help the Utes. They needed to be converted, to be led out of their spiritual darkness into the light through the teachings of the church. She had written the bishop of Utah many times, but he had never answered any of her letters. He would have to answer Father Martin's.

Oh, how she wanted to leave this godless place before its poverty and hopelessness suffocated her. She closed her eyes and prayed.

Maybe life would be better when the work on the ranch was completed and she was back with Raymond. Maybe she wouldn't feel as lonely and depressed then. Maybe. She reached for her pen to write Father Martin.

Awakenings

Despite blistering cold on the night of February 20, 1913, the main street of Vernal, a white settlement twenty-five miles from the Uintah Reservation, had been cluttered with carriages. Mormon families from all over the valley had bundled up and left the warmth of their homes to come to Orpheus Hall to the premiere of an opera written by Zitkala-Ša and Vernal's music teacher, William Hanson. *The Sun Dance* was

William Hanson, ca. 1913. (Courtesy of the Photographic Archives, Harold B. Lee Library, Brigham Young University, Provo, UT.)

a love story set against the backdrop of the most sacred religious experience of the Plains Indians. The plot centered on the commitment of Ohiya, a Sioux man, to complete the

The Sun Dance Opera Company, 1915. (Courtesy of the Photographic Archives, Harold B. Lee Library, Brigham Young University, Provo, UT.)

Sun Dance to prove his worthiness for his beloved, Winona. The hero was named after the Bonnins' son: Ohiya means "winner."

William and Zitkala-Ša had collaborated on every aspect of

the opera. She had taught him the rituals of the Sun Dance—except for the sacred preparations known only to the holy men—and played the chants on her violin. She convinced the Ute religious elders to sing for William, who recorded these melodies on a dictaphone and used them to create arias. Zitkala-Ša acted as his musical conscience: When his music departed too much from traditional Indian melodies, she helped him revise the songs. She rewrote his lyrics so they accurately reflected Indian ideas.

They had divided the job of directing and producing. William had trained the orchestra and chorus of adults and children from Vernal. Zitkala-Ša enlisted Ute friends to create authentic costumes. An elk-tooth wedding dress was donated for Winona. Beaded buckskin leggings were offered for Ohiya, and an assortment of shawls, moccasins, dresses, and belts for the other characters. Zitkala-Ša had convinced Bad Hand and several Ute elders to perform part of the Sun Dance. Originally only two performances were planned, but the demand for seats in Vernal was so great that a third one was given.

There were plans for performances in Utah's capital, Salt Lake City, at Brigham Young University in Provo, and in other small Utah towns.

A scrapbook with newspaper clippings about the premiere pasted neatly into it lay on Zitkala-Ša's piano. There were photographs of Zitkala-Ša and William and reviews praising the production from places as far away as New York City.

It had been a time of triumph for Zitkala-Ša but not for

Raymond. He was worn out from the pettiness and corruption at the Bureau. The acting agent, F. Baker, a greedy, uncaring man, was warring with Raymond's supervisor, Jewell Martin, and Raymond received the fallout from their battles. He needed Zitkala-Ša—he depended on her. She had been with him too little the past year.

Rehearsals had taken her away from the family, and the separation had been especially difficult for him. He felt neglected, and he still felt it even though she was home now. She was always so busy—giving piano or brass lessons to white youngsters on the reservation, holding Saturday-evening musicales or book readings, or playing the organ on Sundays at the Episcopal church.

Raymond's sadness and desperation spilled over into angry words that infected the air. Zitkala-Ša could not believe what she was hearing. Raymond wasn't sure she still loved him. He accused her of paying more attention to Asa Chapman, a clerk at the Agency, than to him.

She exploded. Much of what he was shouting about she had sensed for months. She could understand that he was pained at her being away, but how dare he accuse her of caring for another man. Of course she liked Asa Chapman. He was an interesting, cultured man. Why shouldn't she talk to him about books and music? How could Raymond suggest that anything but friendship was between them? Infuriated, she took Ohiya and stomped out of their cottage.

Rumors that Raymond had beaten her spread through the agency. Baker used the rumors to get back at Martin: He accused him of covering up Raymond's wife-beating, which was a crime in Utah. Distraught and shamed, Zitkala-Ša wrote a priest at the Standing Rock Reservation, pleading for help:

Dear Father Ketcham:

We had an untold unhappiness in our home on account of an unreasonable jealousy that caused my husband to act imprudently. I AM INNOCENT OF ANY IMMORAL ACT. My mistake was in showing too much interest in literary conversations with a man who came frequently to our home.

We have tried to live it down, God only knows how hard. There was no one in our house at the time of our misunderstanding. Yet Mr. Baker, acting agent in the agency, upon hearsay, has written to the Commissioner of Indian Affairs that my husband assaulted me in a jealous rage. This injures Mr. Bonnin's name as well as mine.

It does not seem right that a supervisor should be allowed to damage a subordinate with statements that do not abide strictly to the truth. Mr. Baker has been fighting with Mr. Martin over many things. We have always stood by Mr. Martin, since he is the best person we have had in the ten years we have been here; Mr. Baker felt like hurting us too.

Mr. Bonnin never assaulted me.

I ask that you speak to the commissioner in our behalf. I want the chance to work if a new position of

> *assistant clerk arises. I realize I am asking a great deal,*
> *Father, but I have no other to whom I may turn at this*
> *hour of trial.*

The Bonnins were humiliated by Baker's unfounded smear and by people knowing about their marital difficulties. They talked over what had happened. Zitkala-Ša reassured Raymond of how much she loved him and how indispensable he was to her existence. He apologized for his jealous rage. The tension between them eased, but Zitkala-Ša felt they had to find a way to leave this suffocating place before it destroyed them.

In June she took Ohiya to Nauvoo, Illinois, to enroll him in a Benedictine boarding school. She trusted the Benedictines and wanted her son to have a Catholic education, which he could not get in Utah. That knowledge did not lessen her pain of separating from him.

She continued her journey eastward to visit friends from her conservatory days in Boston. Her train passed through Chicago, and her thoughts turned to Carlos. The last time she had seen him was twelve years ago, when she had stopped in Chicago for a tender few hours. How much she had loved him then.

Over the years, from time to time, she had heard about him. He was married now and still practicing medicine in Chicago. He continued to be outspoken about the need to abolish the Indian Bureau. More and more she agreed with him.

Carlos was a founding member of a new pan-Indian group called the Society of American Indians (SAI). Two letters, with his signature, had come to Utah, inviting the Bonnins to meetings, but they had not been able to attend. Raymond could not get leave from work, and Zitkala-Ša was too busy juggling family responsibilities and the opera.

Self-help through race consciousness, the letters had said. Active membership in the Society of American Indians was limited to persons of Indian blood. Only Indians could assume leadership positions. Only Indians would vote on strategies and actions. A good start, she thought, because the few national organizations dedicated to defending Indian interests were dominated by whites. Years ago she had told Carlos that Indian organizations should not even accept money from whites.

Over two hundred Indians from nations scattered across the United States belonged to the new pan-Indian group. The roster included lawyers, anthropologists, doctors, educators, and Indian Service employees. Most had been educated in boarding schools and were practicing Christians now. Many used both Indian and Euro-American names. Ironically, the boarding schools that had stripped Indians of their diverse cultures had given them a common language, English, which they were using now to unite their peoples.

Zitkala-Ša hoped this group might offer a meaningful way to help Indian peoples and to connect her with the world beyond the reservation. On June 23, 1913, she took a first step by writing Carlos. Hoping to repair the pain and anger between them, she assumed all the blame for their broken engagement:

You had a narrow escape but you escaped because I was not worthy, because I did not recognize true worth at that time. Permit me to say I am one of your admirers and would like to be counted on as one of your friends. I humbly beg your forgiveness for my gross stupidity of former years. I have never passed through Chicago since our last meeting, but I could not go through now without putting forth an effort to reach you—no matter how hard. No matter if you might have refused to see me, I had to try to see you.

She opened herself as she had years before and described her inner turmoil:

I seem to be in a spiritual unrest. I hate this eternal tug-of-war between being wild or becoming civilized. The transition is an endless evolution—that keeps me in continual Purgatory. My duty as mother and wife of course keeps me in the West; but now I can hardly stand the inner spiritual clamor to study, to write—to do more with my music—yet duty first! Rip Van Winkle slept twenty years, but my sleep was disturbed in half that time. I wonder if I may sleep again!

Without explaining why, she asked Carlos not to send her personal mail but to occasionally send his speeches or articles. It had been only three months since the explosion with Raymond. The wound was too recent to risk stirring feelings of jealousy over his former rival.

Zitkala-Ša joined the Society of American Indians and

within a year was asked to serve on its advisory board. Following the Society's commitment to community service, she set up weekly sewing classes in an abandoned warehouse at the agency. Here Ute women sewed for those who didn't have the money to buy clothing or couldn't see well enough anymore to sew. They visited the elderly and sick and brought them food. On cold and rainy issue days the new community house furnished a warm waiting place. At monthly gatherings the women talked about ways to improve life on the reservation. Zitkala-Ša rode to the tipi camps to talk with the women who lived too far away to attend the meetings.

The formation of the Society of American Indians marked the coming together of a new generation of Indians determined to negotiate a better future for all Indians. Zitkala-Ša celebrated the awakening in a poem, tracking the pain of her assimilation and her difficult journey back. She signed the poem Zitkala-Ša, again claiming her public Indian identity and her individuality.

I've lost my long hair; my eagle plumes too.
From you my own people, I've gone astray.
A wanderer now, with nowhere to stay.
The Will-o-the-wisp learning, it brought me rue.
It brings no admittance. Where I have knocked
Some evil imps, hearts, have bolted and locked.
Alone with the night and fearful Abyss
I stand isolated, life gone amiss. . . .

Oh, what am I? Whither bound thus and why?
Is there not a God on whom to rely? . . .

Sweet Freedom. There stood in waiting, a steed
All prancing, well bridled, saddled for speed.
A foot in the stirrup! Off with a bound!
As light as a feather, making no sound.

Away from these worldly ones, let us go,
Along a worn trail, much travelled and,—Lo!
Familiar the scenes that come rushing by.
Now billowy sea and now azure sky.

Hark! Here in the Spirit-world, He doth hold
A village of Indians, camped as of old.
Earth legends by their fires, some did review,
While flowers and trees more radiant grew.

Direct from the Spirit-world came my steed.
The phantom has place in what was all planned.
He carried me back to God and the land
Where all harmony, peace and love are the creed.
In triumph, I cite my Joyous return. . . .

Zitkala-Ša, ca. 1913. (Courtesy of the Photographic Archives, Harold B. Lee Library, Brigham Young University, Provo, UT.)

In 1915 both Raymond's father and Zitkala-Ša's mother died. In October 1916 Zitkala-Ša was elected secretary of the Society of American Indians. The new job necessitated moving to Washington, D.C. In December Bad Hand died. He was buried wearing his war bonnet, wrapped in the U.S. Army coat Raymond had given him the winter they took him into their home. At his side were his pipe, his eagle-feather medicine band, his eagle-wing-bone whistle, and a bouquet of eagle down wrapped in sage.

With Ohiya now settled in boarding school, the Bonnins were free to leave Utah. For Zitkala-Ša, here was her chance to combine her commitment to Indian peoples with the cultural life she loved and needed. For Raymond, moving offered the opportunity to study law. In April 1917 Raymond and Zitkala-Ša left for Washington.

Washington, D.C.
1917–1938

The Peyote Controversy

On February 21, 1918, Zitkala-Ša sat on a hard wooden bench in a windowless room in the Capitol. Sixty years earlier Struck-by-the-Ree had sat on a similar bench and breathed air that had never known freshness as he waited to testify before the Great White Father's representatives. Zitkala-Ša was dressed like her ancestors. She usually wore Indian garments and braided her hair when making public appearances. Non-Indians liked and expected Indians to look like "real" Indians. Unlike her ancestors, who had been forced to capitulate to the Great White Father, she intended to get what she wanted.

It was her first time testifying before a senate subcommittee, and she missed Raymond's being here to lend support. Almost a year ago the United States had entered World War I. Even though Indians were not yet citizens, they were still drafted into the armed forces. At thirty-seven, with a wife and child, Raymond would not have been drafted. But like thousands of other Indians, he volunteered out of patriotic feeling. He was stationed at an Army base in the South, supervising the buying and transporting of food for shipment overseas. Maybe he would get a weekend pass and come back to Washington and they could talk then.

For now she would depend on others. Charles Eastman, the president of the Society of American Indians, was here to testify for her side. Writer, lecturer, and doctor, Eastman was the most well-known college-educated Indian in the United States. Richard Henry Pratt was seated next to Eastman. Twenty years earlier she had attacked Pratt for trying to destroy Indian culture. She had repaired her relationship with him. They did not agree on all issues, but he was a useful ally when they did.

A page called the hearing to order. A bill to regulate liquor and peyote was before Congress. Peyote is a small cactus with a root the size and shape of a radish. Its top—known as a button—is dried and eaten as the central sacrament, like bread and wine, in an Indian religion called peyotism. Peyote users proclaim both its visionary and its medicinal powers: In 1918 there were no sulfa drugs or antibiotics, and many Indians used peyote to help stop the coughing and spitting up of blood from tuberculosis, as well as to relieve other ailments.

Zitkala-Ša was vehemently against peyote being used for any reason even though she had no firsthand knowledge of it. She had never attended or participated in a peyote ceremony, but she believed it was a superstitious ritual. She insisted peyote was an evil, addictive drug that caused people to behave immorally and irresponsibly.

Her hatred of peyote had begun four years before, when Samuel Lone Bear, an Oglala Sioux from South Dakota, came to the Uintah reservation. Lone Bear learned that John Mc Cook, the brother-in-law of the revered Ute chief Ouray, had been ill for many years and had found no relief from either traditional or Western medicine. Lone Bear predicted he would cure him if Mc Cook and others joined him in the ritual of eating the sacred peyote. Mc Cook agreed and, after one meeting, declared himself healed. Soon other respected Ute leaders converted to peyotism. Within a year, half the Utes on the reservation were practicing peyotists.

White Bureau officials jumped to suppress peyotism as they had other Indian rituals. They found fuel for their opposition in the fact that despite Lone Bear's cures and dynamic teachings, he ruthlessly exploited his followers to get money.

Lone Bear's unscrupulous behavior blinded Zitkala-Ša to even considering that peyotism might be a legitimate religious practice. She donned Indian dress and set off to inform women in Utah, Nevada, and Colorado about peyote's "evils." She found a welcome reception in the many women's temperance groups working to stop the sale of alcohol. Her passion convinced them that peyote was as addictive as alcohol. They joined her campaign to get it outlawed, and they succeeded. All three states passed antipeyote laws. Zitkala-Ša intended to be victorious on the federal level too.

"Mr. James Mooney," a senate page called out. A slender fifty-seven-year-old man walked toward the committee. Though she had never met Mooney, she knew he was a highly respected and knowledgeable ethnologist. For twenty-eight years he had studied Indian religious practices. He had attended numerous peyote rituals and had taken peyote at least eight times. Mooney saw the peyote meetings as a unifying experience, a chance for Indians to join with friends and relatives the way they had before federal policy separated them from their kin.

From many years of working among missionaries and Bureau officials, Mooney knew intimately how most despised Indian rituals. He had stopped trying to convince them otherwise but hoped that he might make the senators understand that peyotism was an authentic ritual and that Indians had the inalienable right to worship as they pleased.

Without ever mentioning Zitkala-Ša's name, Mooney opened his testimony by attacking her for a recent interview she had given to the *Washington Times*:

> *This newspaper article is accompanied by a picture of the author who claims to be a Sioux woman in Indian costume. Her dress is a woman's dress from some Southern tribe, as shown by the long fringes. The belt is a Navajo man's belt. The fan is a peyote fan, carried only by men, usually in the peyote ceremony.*
>
> *In the article the woman quotes a man who said that "peyote is used in all-night feasts that lead to the wildest intoxication and orgies in which men, women, and even children take part, to the degradation of their minds."*
>
> *If that were true, it would be good to stamp out these*

*ceremonies, but it is not true. Peyote is not an ordinary
habit, as when men drink whiskey. It is confined to the
religious ceremony or used for medicinal purposes.*

Mooney went on to describe a typical peyote meeting, hoping to educate the senators of its religious importance.

*About every two weeks, late on Saturday afternoon,
Indian families assemble at someone's home. The men
set up a special tipi. The women cook. The children play.
The families eat dinner together. About nine o'clock the
men enter the church or tipi. A fire burns in the center
of the tipi, and a large sacred peyote sits on a little
crescent-shaped mound behind it. The men sit in a circle
around the fire. I have seen as many as thirty men at a
ceremony. After an opening prayer the leader hands out
four peyotes to each man.*

*The men chew one peyote button after another. The
singing begins. There is one regular song at the beginning, one at midnight, one at daylight and one at the
close, but singing goes on all through the night. A drum
and rattle are passed around the circle as different men
sing. The others pray or contemplate, looking toward the
fire and the sacred peyote.*

*At intervals the worshipers eat more peyotes. I have
seen a man eat as many as thirty peyotes. Twenty to forty
is a common number. At midnight they have a kind of
baptismal ceremony. The leader recites a prayer and the*

men sprinkle themselves with spring water. They pray for their friends and for themselves, as we pray.

At daylight they eat special foods prepared by the women, then leave the tipi and chat with their friends until dinner. Dinner is a family affair. In the evening they go home.

There is nothing in this meeting that can be called an orgy. There is nothing that even the most rigid white man could consider immoral. Women and children are never present except when brought in to be prayed for as sick persons.

The next day Zitkala-Ša got her turn to testify. She did not intend to let Mooney's slurs against her go unanswered. It was crucial to convince the senators that she was the expert on peyote, not Mooney. After all, she was the real Indian. Without ever mentioning Mooney's name, she attacked him and all white ethnologists.

Yesterday a gentleman, speaking in favor of peyote, contradicted information from an article in the Sunday Times. *The article quoted an Indian who stated that peyote was used in all-night fetes that led to wild intoxication and to orgies where even children participated.*

The gentleman said that that statement was not true. Ethnologists who visit Indian meetings cannot stay there day after day, month after month, year after year. When they visit, meetings are prearranged for them. I have been

*a schoolteacher too long not to know that when I have
a class recite for a visitor, immediately the air is charged
with a certain restraint. That is human nature. When the
Indians know that an ethnologist is visiting and intends
to write everything down, they naturally cannot help feeling restrained and do not do what they are in the habit
of doing.*

She dramatically refuted Mooney's testimony with hearsay
testimony, a story of a bizarre death that she insisted was
caused by peyote.

*I lived among the Utes of Utah for fourteen years. Dur-
ing those years I visited them in their homes until I knew
them all. I am on good terms with them. I want them
saved if possible. When peyote was first introduced
among the Utes, I saw my friends victimized, and that
hurt my heart. I did not know the technical terms of
peyote; I never saw the thing grow, but common horse
sense told me that the indiscriminate use of a powerful
drug was dead wrong.*

*I know of at least thirty deaths from the use of peyote
among the Utes. A man named Weecheget took an over-
dose and became wild. Before a crowd of whites and
Indians, he tore his clothes off and dove into a deep mud
hole. Then he jumped up to his feet and wildly grabbed
handfuls of the mud and smote himself with it. Before
anyone could help him, he died in a few minutes.*

THE FLIGHT OF RED BIRD

She explained how easily "helpless, downtrodden" peyote users were duped by swindlers such as Samuel Lone Bear.

Samuel Lone Bear, also known as Cactus Pete, was the local supplier of peyote on the Uintah Reservation. He also sold two hundred small crosses of very inferior material at a dollar each. He told his victims to put the magic crosses away and not to wear them but to look at them once in a while. If they saw that the cross was tarnishing, as of course it was bound to, it was an evil omen, a sign of their approaching death, only to be healed by eating more peyote. Cactus Pete knew that the fear of approaching death would make the Indian willing to pay any price for peyote treatment or do anything for him.

These crosses could not have cost over ten cents. Pete sold them for a dollar each. He made one hundred eighty dollars on a twenty-dollar investment, to say nothing of playing upon the Indians' superstition.

He told Indians who owned cattle that they need not trouble themselves to ride to the hills to watch their stock. All they had to do was to stay at home, and with the peyote in their hands ask about the cattle, and the peyote would tell them if anyone was trying to steal the cattle.

She concluded with a dramatic warning:

> *Human nature is the same regardless of color. This habit of using peyote is not going to be limited to the red man alone. We already see it spreading out among the white men. Soldiers on the Texas border are using it, and I have heard of white people substituting peyote for opium. Schoolchildren and babies, of course, use it as well as adults.*
>
> *This menace is going to spread like wildfire. We need now to protect all Americans by quenching this little spark.*

Twenty-three people appeared before the committee. The roster of Indians and non-Indians included well-known reformers, ethnologists, doctors, and Indian Bureau officials. Fifteen people, many of whom were peyotists, testified that peyote was nonaddictive and an essential part of a religious ritual. They emphasized its medicinal value: It relieved symptoms of tuberculosis and rheumatism and helped alcoholics stop drinking. Eight people spoke against peyote. All condemned it, though none had any personal experience with it or its use in the ritual ceremony.

The senators on the committee believed the antipeyotists and recommended passing the bill, but when the full Senate voted, it did not pass. Over the next three years three other similar bills came up before Congress. None passed. The antipeyotists continued their state-by-state campaigns, and by 1923 fourteen states had antipeyote laws.

Eight months after the first congressional hearings, a charter for the Native American Church was registered in Oklahoma. Hoping to protect peyotism under the First Amendment right of freedom of worship, James Mooney helped draft this document establishing it as an official church.

Zitkala-Ša was outraged by Mooney's action. She wrote to Bruce Kinney, General Superintendent of the American Baptist Home Mission Society, and to Captain Richard Henry Pratt that Mooney should be fired from his job with the Bureau of Ethnology. Pratt agreed and dashed off letters to various senators and federal officials stating that Mooney "never was anything but a curse to the Indian." Their vindictive campaign did not succeed in getting Mooney fired, but he was barred from visiting Indian reservations in Oklahoma. Mooney died three years after the 1918 hearings, never finishing his life's study on the peyote religion.

Arguments over peyotism within the Society of American Indians pitted Indian against Indian. At its 1919 conference, the peyote majority elected Thomas Sloan as president.

Zitkala-Ša was nominated to continue as secretary and treasurer. She refused: Her doctor had told her to stop working or she would not recover from her frequent fevers, shaking chills, and debilitating flus. There is no doubt that her health was poor, but it is more likely that she resigned because she knew that with a peyotist as president, she would have little power within the organization.

"Oklahoma's Poor Rich Indians"

In December 1923 the winds in eastern Oklahoma blew cold and hard, like those on the Dakota prairie, but nothing else in this landscape bore any resemblance to the northern plains. Gone were the trees and the grass, burned to make way for the giant oil riggers that tapped the black river from the once-green earth. In the scarred fields tall wooden derricks roared out blue flames, as if acknowledging the pain they were imposing on the ground below. In 1905 oil had been discovered here on Indian-owned land, and with it the possibility of untold wealth for Indians.

The Osages were the richest people, per capita, in the world. Newspapers documented their extravagant spending sprees. White Americans gobbled up the photographs of their glittering jewels and furs, expensive cars, and luxurious mansions.

Zitkala-Ša was in Oklahoma investigating reports that Cherokee, Choctaw, Creek, Chickasaw, and Seminole Indians here had been swindled out of millions of dollars. She was working for the General Federation of Women's Clubs, one of the most prominent women's organizations in the United States. Two years before, at the Federation's annual meeting, she had given an impassioned speech about what life was like for most Indians in the United States. The audience, almost all white women, was so moved by the inequities and corruption that she described that the Federation immediately established an Indian Welfare Committee and hired her to work for it.

For five weeks she and Matthew K. Sniffen, secretary of the Indian Rights Organization, and Charles H. Fabens, lawyer for the American Indian Defense Organization, drove up dirt roads into the hills and sat on ramshackle porches and in dilapidated shacks talking with Indian people of all ages. They attended hearings in dreary courtrooms and pored over thousands of pages of legal documents in over 14,000 probate cases.

They were horrified by what they read and heard. In the past twenty years at least 59,000 Indians had been tricked and forced into selling oil-rich lands to white Oklahomans. Young girls were kidnapped and raped. Men were plied with liquor and threatened. Most Indians who still owned land had no control over it or their money. Local judges had declared them "incompetent" and appointed "guardians" for them. Indians were dying of malnourishment and neglect while their white guardians spent their money on lavish houses and cars.

Zitkala-Ša, Fabens, and Sniffen documented the ruthless exploitation in a thirty-nine-page pamphlet, *Oklahoma's Poor*

Rich Indians. They condemned the guardian system and recommended that control over Indian property be given back to federal officials. To dramatize the injustices, Zitkala-Ša documented the lives of some "poor rich" Indians, such as Ledcie Stechi:

> Little Ledcie Stechi, a Choctaw minor, seven years old, owned rich oil property in McCurtain County. She lived with her old grandmother in a small shack back in the hills about two and a half miles from Smithville. They lived in dire poverty, without proper food or clothing and surrounded by filth and dirt. Ledcie inherited lands from her mother, including twenty acres which became valuable oil property.
>
> After the discovery of the oil, her uncle, who was her guardian, was induced to resign through a combination of force, persuasion, and an offer of a reward which he never got. Mr. Jordan Whiteman, owner of the First National Bank of Idabel, whose attorney was instrumental in her uncle's resignation, was appointed guardian. During the time of Mr. Whiteman's appointment, July 1921 until 1923, Ledcie and her grandmother were in a semi-starving condition. Once a week the old grandmother walked to Smithville to buy food on the monthly credit of $15 allowed by Mr. Whiteman, at Blake's store. They had no conveyance. Sometimes the grandmother was too tired to walk back. Then she hired someone to take her home, which cost fifty or sixty cents. The guardian did

nothing to make them more comfortable or to educate the little Indian heiress.

In the fall of 1922 the guardian attempted to sell ten acres of Ledcie's oil land, appraised at $90,000, for $2,000. This attempt was defeated, and with the result that Ledcie Stechi's monthly allowance was increased to $200, from which the guardian allowed the child and grandmother a credit of $15 monthly at a local store. In April 1923 they were brought to the County seat. The rich little Choctaw girl, with her feeble grandmother, came carrying their clothes, a bundle of faded rags in a flour sack. Ledcie was dirty, filthy, and covered with vermin. She weighed about forty-seven pounds.

A medical examination showed she was undernourished and poisoned by malaria. After five weeks of medical treatment and nourishment, she gained eleven pounds. Her health improved. She was placed by an employee of the Indian Service in an Indian school. Her guardian, evidently fearing to lose his grasp on his ward, demanded the child, and she was returned to his custody. The last time the aged grandmother saw Ledcie, and only for a few minutes, was on the twelfth of July.

On August 14 word was brought to the hills that Ledcie was dead. There had been no word of her illness. The following day, at dawn, parties of grafters arrived at the grandmother's hovel in the hills and harassed the bereaved old woman about the disposal of Ledcie's valuable properties. Rival speculators went over with the body of Ledcie. Some sent flowers to be placed on her grave, hoping to play upon her grandmother's heart, for she was the sole heir to Ledcie's vast estate.

The grandmother wailed over the little dead body. In vain she asked for an autopsy, believing Ledcie had been poisoned. "No use. Bury the body," commanded the legal guardian. The Court appointed a guardian for the grandmother, against her vehement protest.

As the widow of an Osage man, Martha Axe Roberts was entitled to $15,000 a year. But her guardian, L. T. Hill, gave her only $1.50 a week. She fled his control and took her two children to live near her parents. Hill refused to give her any money until she returned to Osage County. He tracked her down. One day she returned home to find her car and all her furniture gone. Hill placed a notice in the newspaper warning people not to give her credit. When Martha's fourteen-month-old baby became sick, she telephoned Hill for money for food and medical care. He refused. The baby died.

Martha went to court to get Hill removed as her guardian. Zitkala-Ša attended the hearing and described how Oklahoma justice worked:

Martha's attorney presented government records showing her enrollment in the Osage tribe, which entitled her to her dead husband's inheritance. Hill's lawyer, Sturgill, a former judge who had appointed Hill as Martha's guardian, objected to the evidence. His objections were upheld by the county judge and stricken from the record. It was next to impossible for Martha's lawyer to submit any evidence for her. The court stenographer forgot to take down his statements until he requested her to do so. But whenever Hill's lawyer spoke, the judge's hearing improved.

The Court would not hear the story of Martha's deprivations and poverty, but much went into its records about her father being a worthless drunkard and that Martha had no sense of the value of money, nor of right and wrong, and that she was crazy. Within a half hour the Court dismissed the case.

I felt an overwhelming indignation at the legal helplessness of a poor, rich Indian woman. Yet there was a question in my mind if Martha was mentally unbalanced because of the strain and humiliation of her situation. Perhaps there might be some foundation for this official statement against her that she was crazy. I went to meet her.

She is a gentle, bright-eyed woman, very intelligent, though unlettered. She told me that Hill had a store in Hominy to which he limited all her purchases. He sold her shopworn blankets that had holes in them at full price and refused to exchange them when she protested. When she wanted to buy a Singer sewing machine, he told her she had no money. But he bought her, out of her own funds, an expensive Packard car, and submitted to the Court a gas bill for eight months amounting to $2,750. Judge Sturgill, then on the bench, approved it. Mr. Hill's father-in-law sells gasoline.

Mr. Hill is trying to force her to leave her parents. She wants to live among her people, whose language she speaks. Martha has more than enough means for herself and her child.

I met her father, John Washington, who is a bricklayer and stone cutter. He is well informed in practical business methods and has a keen memory. He did not deny the charge that he uses intoxicating liquors, but told me of many occasions when Mr. Hill supplied him with his whiskey in the name of friendship.

I called at the Farmers State Bank in Vinita and asked the cashier, Mr. Martin, if he knew John Washington. He said, "Yes." Mr. Martin was born and raised there and knew everybody. I asked him if the charge that John Washington was a worthless drunk was true. He said, "I have never seen him drunk. On the contrary I consider Martha and her father intelligent above the average Indian."

The personal vignettes and statistics in *Oklahoma's Poor Rich Indians* shocked and horrified even cynical lawmakers. The pamphlet spurred a meeting of four hundred Indians in Tulsa, where copies of it were handed out and read. A statewide protective organization was formed. L. T. Hill retaliated and had a warrant issued against Zitkala-Ša for criminal libel.

Nine months later congressional hearings were held in Oklahoma. People who had cooperated with Zitkala-Ša, Fabens, and Sniffen were badgered and belittled when they testified. Zitkala-Ša did not attend the hearings. All during Sniffen's three-day testimony, Oklahoma officials and oil-company representatives attacked him for misrepresenting the facts.

The congressmen concluded that the pamphlet was filled with distortions and lies and publicly censured the three investigators. Making a few concessions to the charges in the report, they did acknowledge that there were some corrupt guardians and agreed that control over Indian property should be taken away from local guardians and given back to federal officials.

The whitewash didn't take. Oklahoma newspapers declared the hearings a sham. The state bar association denounced the unscrupulous lawyer-guardians. Oklahoma state lawmakers set limits on guardian fees, but many guardians found ways around the law to continue swindling their wards of money. The federal government brought corruption charges against twenty-four guardians, but all escaped punishment by settling out of court.

Why didn't Zitkala-Ša go to Oklahoma to testify? *Oklahoma's Poor Rich Indians* never mentioned the early-1920s Oklahoma spree of murders of oil-rich Osage men, women, and children, which local newspapers referred to as the "Reign of Terror." In 1923 an FBI investigation uncovered twenty-four bodies in fields and ravines, on roadsides, or in the debris of bombed-out homes. As many as sixty people, three percent of the Osage nation, had been murdered. Within days of their deaths, their oil shares were transferred to white Oklahomans instead of to their survivors. Zitkala-Ša, Fabens, and Sniffen knew about these murders, for they had been front-page news.

Probably Zitkala-Ša did not go to Oklahoma to testify because she feared for her life. As an Indian she knew it was worth little there. It was not unrealistic to think that if she returned, she might be murdered for her part in exposing the vicious corruption.

Tricksters

Oran Curry and the other members of the Ute tribal council carefully explained the latest case of Bureau corruption on the Uintah Reservation to the U.S. senator. The Utes had still not seen a penny of the $3-million settlement from their Colorado land. Without their permission, the Uintah superintendent had used the money to build two unneeded steel bridges and to pave roads that benefited only white settlers on the reservation. Oran insisted the superintendent be dismissed immediately and that all the money be returned to his people.

The senator suggested they tell their story to the House Committee on Indian Affairs. Zitkala-Ša saw Oran's hopeful face. She was not as hopeful. Most *wašíčun* did not yet know how to listen. She had attended too many hearings where representatives had humiliated Indians by talking to them as if they were little children at a school drill.

In this winter of 1930 life was especially desperate for Indians. Since the stock market crash on October 29, 1929, an economic depression had gripped the nation. Banks had failed. Businesses had crumbled. Twelve million Americans were out of work. President Herbert Hoover had said, "We have now passed the worst." Obviously he hadn't seen the soup kitchens and breadlines in the cities or read the government reports bulging with statistics about the deplorable living conditions of most Indians.

Zitkala-Ša didn't need to read government reports. Piled on her desk were letters from Indian veterans who weren't receiving their benefits, from sick people who had no money for medicine or food, and from parents whose children had been taken by force and shipped off to boarding schools.

She had crisscrossed the country giving over four hundred lectures on the rightness of all Indians being granted citizen-

Gertrude Bonnin at the Catholic Sioux Congress, Pine Ridge, South Dakota, 1922. (Courtesy of the Marquette University Archives.)

ship and control of their own lives. Citizenship had come two years ago, but it was meaningless. The reservations were still prisons with invisible walls dominated by federal officials who controlled Indian lives and money.

Four years earlier she and Raymond had formed their own organization, the National Council of American Indians (NCAI), hoping to unite Indians into a political force. Perhaps then politicians would help them.

A meeting to negotiate a movie contract with the Bonnins and members of the Ute nation. *Bottom row:* the Bonnins. *Top row, left to right:* movie producer; Ohiya Bonnin (?); Oran Curry; John Pawwinnee, leader of the Uncompahgre band of the Utes; Sapanis Cuch, Whiteriver Council member; unidentified person; Roy Smith, Uintah Council member. (Courtesy of Richard Curry.)

She was an old hand now at testifying before Congress, but it was as impossible for her and Raymond to track every relevant piece of legislation as it was for them to solve the problems in the letters. Most lawmakers did not understand or care about Indian people. Many said one thing to Zitkala-Ša in private meetings but showed another face among their colleagues. Zitkala-Ša was not surprised.

She was always on her guard with government officials. Her mother had taught her to look carefully, "take in all in a single glance." She remembered an Iktomi story that warned her what happens to those who foolishly trust the untrustworthy:

Iktomi sat in his tipi thinking, *Where will I get my next meal?* He put on his beaded deerskin jacket, deerskin leggings with long fringes on the sides, and beaded moccasins. He parted his long black hair in the middle and wrapped it with red bands. Then he painted his face red and yellow and drew big black rings around his eyes. Now he looked like a proper Dakota man.

Suddenly he rushed out, dragging his blanket. Quickly spreading it on the ground, he tore up tall grass and tossed it into the blanket. Tying all four corners of the blanket together in a knot, he threw the bundle of grass over his shoulder. Snatching up a slender stick from a willow tree near his tipi, he started off with a hop and a leap.

Soon he came to the edge of a great level stretch of

land. On the hilltop he paused for breath. With wicked smacks of his dry parched lips, as if tasting some tender meat, he looked straight into space toward the marshy river bottom. With a thin palm shading his eyes from the western sun, he peered far away into the lowlands, munching his cheeks. "Ah-ha!" he grunted.

A group of ducks were dancing and feasting in the marshes. With wings outspread, tip to tip, they moved up and down in a large circle. Within the ring, around a small drum, sat the singers, nodding their heads and blinking their eyes.

Iktomi bent himself over like an old man exhausted by the burden of a heavy bundle. With his willow cane he propped himself up as he staggered down the footpath toward the ducks.

"Ho! Who is there?" called out a curious old duck, bobbing up and down in the circular dance. The drummers stretched their necks until they strangled their song for a look at the stranger.

"Ho, old fellow, pray tell us what you carry in your blanket. Do not hurry off!" urged a singer.

"Show us what is in your blanket!" cried out other voices.

"My friends," Iktomi said, "I do not want to spoil your dance, for you would stop dancing if you knew what is in my blanket."

This reply broke up the circle. The ducks crowded about Iktomi.

"We must know what is in your blanket!" they

shouted in both his ears. Some even brushed their wings against the mysterious bundle.

"My friends, 'tis only a pack of songs."

"Oh, let us hear your songs!"

At length Iktomi consented to sing. With great care, he laid his bundle on the ground. "I will first build a round house, for I never sing in the open air." Quickly he bent green willow sticks, planting the ends of each stick into the earth. He covered the sticks with reeds and grasses. Soon the straw hut was ready. One by one the fat ducks waddled in through a small opening, which was the only entrance. Beside the door Iktomi stood smiling as the ducks strutted into the hut.

In a strange low voice Iktomi began his tunes. The ducks sat in a circle about the mysterious singer. It was dim in the hut, for Iktomi had covered up the small entranceway. His voice swelled and swelled until it boomed. The startled ducks sat uneasily on the ground. Iktomi changed his tune into a minor strain.

He sang, "With eyes closed, you must dance. He who dares to open his eyes will forever have red eyes."

Up rose the circle of ducks, and holding their wings close against their sides, they began to dance with closed eyes to the rhythm of Iktomi's song and drum. Iktomi ceased to beat his drum and began to sing louder and faster. He seemed to be moving about in the center of the circle. No duck dared blink. Up and down! They hopped round and round in that blind dance.

At length one dancer opened his eyes. "Oh! Oh!" he

squawked in awful terror. "Run! Fly! Iktomi is twisting our heads and breaking our necks!"

The other ducks opened their eyes. There beside Iktomi's bundle of songs lay half of their crowd—flat on their backs.

Out the rest flew through the opening made by the first duck as he rushed forth with his alarm. When they were high enough in the sky to feel safe, they looked at each other and saw that Iktomi's warning had proven true. Their eyes were red.

"Ah-ha!" laughed Iktomi, untying the four corners of his blanket. "I shall be hungry no more." He trudged home with the nice fat ducks in his blanket. He left the straw hut for the rains and winds to pull down.

He kindled a large fire. He planted sharp-pointed sticks around the leaping flames. On each stake he fastened a duck. A few he buried under the ashes to bake. He set a huge seashell under each roasting duck. He muttered, "The sweet fat oozing out will taste well with the hard-cooked breasts."

Heaping more willows upon the fire, Iktomi sat down on the ground. Now and then he sniffed impatiently the savory odor. The brisk wind which had stirred his fire now played with the squeaky old willow tree beside his wigwam. From side to side the tree was swaying and crying in an old man's voice, "Help! I'm breaking!"

Iktomi shrugged his shoulders but did not once take his eyes off the ducks. The dripping of the amber oil into the pearly dishes, drop by drop, pleased his hungry eyes. Still the old tree man called out for help.

"He! What sound is it that makes my ear ache!" exclaimed Iktomi, holding a hand on his ear.

He rose and looked around. The squeaking came from the tree. He began climbing the tree to find the disagreeable sound. He placed his foot on a cracked limb without seeing it. Just then a fierce wind rushed by and pressed the limb's broken edges together around his foot, then up around his body. "My foot is crushed!" he howled. In vain he pulled and puffed to free himself.

He spied through his tears a pack of gray wolves roaming over the level lands. Waving his hands, he called in his loudest voice, "He! Gray wolves, don't you come here! I'm caught fast in the tree and my duck feast is getting cold."

The leader of the pack turned to his comrades and said, "Ah! Hear the foolish fellow. He says he has a duck feast to be eaten. Let us hurry there for our share!"

From the tree, Iktomi watched the hungry wolves eat up his nicely browned fat ducks. He heard them crack the small round bones with their strong long teeth and eat out the oily marrow. Pain shot up from his foot through his whole body. Real tears washed brown streaks across his red-painted cheeks.

Smacking their lips, the wolves began to leave, when Iktomi cried out, "At least you have left the rest of my food under the ashes!"

THE FLIGHT OF RED BIRD

The wolves laughed and pawed out the remaining ducks with such haste that a cloud of ashes rose like gray smoke over them.

"Hin-hin-hin," moaned Iktomi, when the wolves had scampered off. All too late the sturdy breeze returned and pulled apart the broken edges of the tree and freed Iktomi.

The Iktomi stories Zitkala-Ša had heard as a child taught her how human beings behaved and warned her to always "keep her eyes open." She had temporarily forgotten that, when the white men with the large hats told her about the wonders awaiting her in the Red Apple Country. But once she realized she had been tricked, she fought back. At boarding school, learning that her hair was going to be cut, she had turned school routine upside down making everyone search for her. When punished for misconduct and ordered to mash turnips in a glass jar, she was "so obedient" that she shattered the jar and ruined the turnips. Now, in Washington, she played the game of politics, using statistics, persuasion, and persistence to pressure lawmakers to rectify injustices.

She hid her Indian identity when necessary and exploited it when beneficial. Government officials and politicians knew her by her Euro-American names, Gertrude Bonnin or Mrs. Raymond Bonnin, but when appearing before Congress, she donned traditional dress to remind the representatives that she was an "authentic" Indian. She claimed to be a full-blooded Yankton, which was not true, and a granddaughter of Sitting

Bull. The second claim impressed them even more but it was absurd, for Sitting Bull was a Hunkpapa and if she was his granddaughter she could not be of pure Yankton blood. She knew most Congress members lumped all Indians together and did not distinguish among the various tribes in the Sioux federation.

Though neither claim was true, Zitkala-Ša saw herself as continuing the great Sioux warrior tradition. She defended her people with new weapons learned from her enemy—her pen, the English language, and her organizational persistence.

Despair

In the next seven years Zitkala-Ša and Raymond traveled for five months each year from reservation to reservation, gathering evidence of the ongoing injustices toward Native Americans. The rest of the year they lived in Washington, D.C., meeting with legislators and pressing for laws to help Indians gain control of their lives. Fragments in Zitkala-Ša's diary kept from 1936–1938 reveal that her health had greatly deteriorated from the exhaustion of constant travel, and that her frustration and disappointment over being unable to effect change had turned to bitterness.

The summer of 1936 had brought the usual stifling heat and wet air to the capital area. Zitkala-Ša had stayed home from the office, hoping for quiet and comfort. The house was weighed down with an uncomfortable silence. Her body throbbed with pain, with the years of struggle, of speaking out and not being heard. She felt as if she were being smothered. No use telling anyone how she felt. Not even Raymond.

She didn't think he would understand. Her only confidant now was her diary.

Maybe it was another flu attack coming on. Her sixty-year-old body had little resistance after three bouts these last five months. The past year had brought more frequent and severe fevers and chills. Many nights she woke up coughing and choking, panicked that she would not be able to breathe.

Illness stalked their family. The trachoma that Raymond had contracted at boarding school continually flared up. And their dear Ohiya, now thirty-three years old, had such severe diabetes that he was in and out of the hospital. Even with insulin the doctors didn't seem to be able to control his disease. His wife, Elsie, was also sick, but the doctors had not yet diagnosed exactly what was wrong. No wonder Ohiya was depressed.

He kept talking about returning to Utah to work for the Indian Service and raise horses. No doubt Zitkala-Ša's four grandchildren would be better off there than in the East, and Elsie and Ohiya would be among loving friends like Oran Curry and his wife, Della. But how could Ohiya manage a job plus the strenuous work on a ranch? Elsie was too sick to help him. And where would he get the money to buy land? She and Raymond didn't have any to give.

Two years ago, when they had visited Chicago, their two eldest grandchildren had been out of control, in perpetual motion, running and screaming about the apartment. Ohiya was a bundle of nerves, and Elsie couldn't cope with even the simplest housekeeping tasks. Zitkala-Ša and Raymond had decided then to take the two oldest boys to live with them, but she had not been prepared for how difficult it would be.

Raymie was thirteen now; Joseph was ten. They constantly quarreled and competed for attention. Recently she had slapped Raymie and struck him with a switch. Her behavior horrified her, but she was tired of playing policeman, tired of trying to train these hardheaded boys. She was too old to be a mother and too old to be poor.

Her diamond engagement ring sat in a pawn shop in a glass case along with the jewelry of other desperate people. The pawn ticket was in her bureau drawer waiting to be redeemed, but with bill collectors hounding them, she doubted she would be wearing her ring soon. Would she ever wear it again?

Where would they turn when the money from the ring ran out? Gracie, her dear friend from her years at the conservatory in Boston, had a generous husband who had lent them money more than once. How many more times could they ask him for help?

When she and Raymond had started the NCAI, they had assumed it would be supported by membership dues. Annual dues were only a dollar, but most Indians on reservations could not afford even that dollar, and finding wealthy contributors had proven impossible. The plight of Indians was not a popular cause.

She still made some money lecturing to women's groups and literary societies, but speaking engagements meant lugging her buckskin dress on the train to Baltimore or New York City. She no longer had the strength or desire to dress up like a "real Indian."

Raymond worked now for the law firm representing the Utes in their land-claim case against the federal government. He was confident they would win. His share of the judgment would be at least $100,000. When . . . if . . . Such cases dragged on for years.

She had dreamed of uniting Indians into a political force, and she had failed despite all her hard work these past twelve years, despite all the testifying before Congress, despite all the visits west to the reservations. She did not regret that she had tried, for she had learned much in the struggle; but she wondered if it would ever really change. It felt too strenuous to even remember what she had accomplished.

Some Bureau superintendents on reservations were as hostile as officials had been when she was born. Some forbade her and Raymond to even hold meetings. Some tried to poison people's minds against them. Sometimes they succeeded. The Yankton superintendent was particularly vicious: He had refused to distribute food and clothing intended for the needy to the relatives of anyone who belonged to the NCAI.

Everywhere she turned, she felt betrayed. Even people she thought were friends had turned out not to be. For twenty-five years she had worked with John Collier, drawing up legislation and lobbying Congress. She had served as his hostess at literary and musical evenings at his home. Now he was Commissioner of Indian Affairs. Yes, they disagreed over certain policies, but people with strong ideas often disagreed and still respected each other and worked together.

She had assumed Collier would hire her and Raymond in his administration. He knew there were no two people more concerned with the welfare of Indians. But all Collier had offered was an insult—a superintendency in New Mexico for Raymond, at a salary much less than what the previous white superintendent had gotten.

Dear, gentle Raymond. He sensed her growing despair and tried to encourage her by reminding her of their successes. How could he call them successful when every day brought more desperate letters from Indians, more unsolvable problems to her desk?

Maybe the answer was to leave Washington and go back to South Dakota. No more days in airless, dreary committee rooms. No more tedious, unfruitful sessions with unsympathetic lawmakers. No more watching her tongue so as not to offend or holding back what she really felt.

Her happiest times were always the summers on the Yankton Reservation surrounded by kinfolk. She was nourished by the rolling green hills of the prairie, the endless expanse of blue sky, and the long stretch of the muddy Missouri. There was so much love and laughter with David and Victoria and their children. And listening to the elders, like Grandma Smoke, tell the old stories exhilarated her as much now as it had when she was a child. Maybe she could convince Ohiya to move to South Dakota instead of Utah. It could be as in the *tiyóśpaye*.

Her people needed her. David was ill and didn't have enough money to care for his family. This past winter on the Yankton Reservation some people had had so little money, they could not buy fuel. To keep from freezing, they had burned the furniture in their homes. If the summer drought continued, there would be no harvest at Yankton. The Catholic church had set up an emergency soup kitchen, but it didn't have enough money to feed every needy person. She shuddered. What would this winter bring?

The feeling of being smothered was coming on again. She was slipping—she had no anchor, nothing to hold on to. What could she do to stop it? Pray? No, that would be pointless, for she no longer believed in the power of Jesus. She no longer went to church, for she could not bear the petty interpretations of the Great Spirit offered by small-minded church officials. Her heart was the only altar for her soul to worship the Infinite Creator.

Maybe she would nap. It might help fight off the flu . . . if this was the flu. Play the piano? That always nourished her. No, better yet. In her drawer were several strands of beads that had been broken for months. She would restring them and wear them this evening and surprise Raymond and the boys with wild rice and pork chops for dinner. After dinner she would tell Joseph and Raymie the story of how the muskrat outwitted Iktomi when he was too greedy to share his food. The boys needed to learn to listen, so that when spring arrived on the prairie, they would hear the meadowlarks sing.

Red Bird's Flight

On January 26, 1938, Zitkala-Ša died in despair, in Washington, D.C., questioning the worth of her life work. But others did not. At her funeral John Collier and other important advocates for Indian rights praised her commitment and accomplishments.

Red Bird was a warrior for Indian justice. She never lost sight of the strength and vision of her people, a people who had never been passive in protecting themselves from white encroachment and had resisted since their first encounters with the Europeans. She worked relentlessly to effect change for Native Americans, and she had her share of successes, big and small. She represented Indians from over thirty-five nations, including Apaches, Arapahoes, Cheyennes, Kiowas, Navajos, Osages, Pueblos, Poncas, and the Sioux. She gave dignity to individuals by answering every letter asking for help. No problem was too insignificant for her to tackle.

She used her pen, her voice, and legal action to attack and dismantle federal policies that controlled Indian lives. She stumped the campaign trail in Oklahoma and defeated the reelection of Congressman John W. Harreld, who had done nothing to protect the Indians in the oil scandals. She lobbied Congress to amend the Oil Leasing Act so the Navajos received 100% of their money, instead of 62%. She helped the Yanktons regain the right to mine pipestone for their sacred pipes at the quarry in Minnesota as guaranteed in the Treaty of 1858. She worked to rescue the $30-million Flathead water-power site in Montana from white control. Despite her differences with and bitterness toward Indian Commissioner John Collier, he introduced many reforms that they had fought for together, such as ending the disastrous policy of allotment and encouraging tribal government. And in 1950, twelve years after Zitkala-Ša's death and eight years after Raymond's death, the Utes were finally awarded $31 million in their land claim case against the federal government.

Red Bird's flight was never completed. She continually circled overhead, looking for a place to land and nest. She never found a resting place, either on the reservation or in the cities of the East. She never resolved the split within her between the Indian world and the white world. The generosity of Indian communal life highlighted the competitiveness and greed of the white world, but returning to the old ways was impossible. The "artificial" world provided satisfactions she could no longer live without. By dedicating her life to serving Indian peoples, she found a way to bridge both worlds. It was an uneasy solution at best, but it gave her life meaning.

In devoting her life to the idea of a pan-Indian organization

Zitkala-Ša, ca. 1913. (Courtesy of the Photographic Archives, Harold B. Lee Library, Brigham Young University, Provo, UT.)

to unite all Indian peoples, Zitkala-Ša paved the way for other Native Americans to take flight. Her legacy reverberates today as Indian activists continue the struggle for self-determination.

IMPORTANT DATES

1830. The Indian Removal Act allows the forced removal of Eastern Indians from their homelands to lands west of the Mississippi River.

circa 1835. Ellen Taté Iyóhiwin is born.

April 19, 1858. Yankton tribal leaders sign the Treaty of Washington that establishes the Yankton Reservation.

February 22, 1876. Zitkala-Ša is born to Taté Iyóhiwin and her third husband, Felker. At this time only four of her eight older children are still living: Peter, Edward, and Henry St. Pierre, from her first husband; and David Simmons, from her second husband.

June 25, 1876. The Sioux and the Cheyenne defeat General George Custer and his troops at the Battle of Greasy Grass or Little Bighorn, Montana.

1878–1881. David Simmons attends Hampton Normal Institute in Virginia. He returns to the Yankton Reservation and works for the Bureau of Indian Affairs, first as issue clerk, then as assistant farming instructor.

1883. The publication of Helen Hunt Jackson's *Century of Dishonor*, which documents how the United States repeatedly broke its treaties with the Indians, spurs the formation of the Indian Rights Association (1882), the Women's National Indian Association (1883), Friends of the Indian (1883).

1882–1884. Zitkala-Ša attends day school on the Yankton Reservation.

February 1884–February 1887. Zitkala-Ša attends White's Manual Labor Institute in Wabash, Indiana.

1887. In an effort to break up tribal unity, Congress passes the Dawes Act, which divides reservation land into individual plots.

February 1887–September 1889. Zitkala-Ša returns to live with her mother.

1889. South Dakota becomes a state.

April 1889. Oklahoma is opened to non-Indian settlement.

Fall 1889–June 1890. Zitkala-Ša attends the Santee School.

December 15, 1890. Sitting Bull is murdered by Indian police sent to arrest him. On December 29 three hundred Sioux men, women, and children are massacred at Wounded Knee in South Dakota.

June 1890–February 1891. Zitkala-Ša stays with her mother on the Yankton Reservation.

February 1891–June 28, 1895. Zitkala-Ša attends White's Manual Labor Institute again.

September 1895–June 1897. Zitkala-Ša attends Earlham College in Richmond, Indiana.

February 1896. Zitkala-Ša wins second prize in Indiana State Oratorical Contest.

◆ ◆ *Important Dates* ◆ ◆

July 1897–January 1899. Zitkala-Ša teaches at the U.S. Indian Industrial School in Carlisle, Pennsylvania.

January 1899–May 1901. Zitkala-Ša attends the New England Conservatory of Music in Boston, Massachusetts. In 1900 *Atlantic Monthly* publishes her reminiscences; in 1901 Ginn and Company publishes *Old Indian Legends*.

June 1901–September 1902. Zitkala-Ša works in South Dakota as issue clerk at Standing Rock Reservation. On August 10, 1902, she and Raymond Bonnin are married.

1903 Ohiya Bonnin is born.

1903–1916. The Bonnins live on the Uintah Reservation in Utah. From March 1905 to November 1906 Zitkala-Ša teaches at the boarding school on this reservation.

1906. The Burke Act eliminates a twenty-five-year trust allowing white homesteaders to buy land on reservations. Citizenship for Native Americans, already acquired through treaties and other legal mechanisms, is withdrawn until individuals receive titles to their land.

Winter 1908–Spring 1909. The Bonnins are at the Standing Rock Reservation in South Dakota.

October 12, 1911. Over fifty Indian men and women attend the first meeting of the Society of American Indians.

February 20, 1913. *The Sun Dance* premieres in Vernal, Utah. More performances are given in December 1913 and February 1914 in Salt

Lake City, in May–December 1914 at Brigham Young University in Provo, and in other Utah towns.

June 1913. Ohiya is enrolled at a Benedictine school in Nauvoo, Illinois.

1914. Zitkala-Ša joins the advisory board of Society of American Indians. World War I begins. The United States enters the war on April 6, 1917.

1915. Zitkala-Ša's mother dies.

1917–1938. Raymond and Zitkala-Ša live in Washington, D.C.

1916 to 1919. Zitkala-Ša is secretary of the Society of American Indians and editor of its publication, *American Indian Magazine*. Raymond enlists in the Army. On August 18, 1919, he is honorably discharged.

1920. The Nineteenth Amendment to the U.S. Constitution, giving women the vote, is ratified. Congress passes a law permitting Indian veterans to apply for citizenship.

1920–1923. Zitkala-Ša works as investigator and lecturer for the Indian Welfare Committee of the General Federation of Women's Clubs. She co-authors *Oklahoma's Poor Rich Indians*.

1921. Ginn and Company publishes Zitkala-Ša's *American Indian Stories*.

June 2, 1924. The Individual Citizenship Act grants citizenships to all noncitizen Indians born within the United States.

1926–1938. Zitkala-Ša and Raymond form the National Council of American Indians (NCAI) and become perpetual lobbyists at Congressional hearings. They travel as much as five months a year to Midwestern and Western reservations organizing local chapters.

1933–1945. Franklin Delano Roosevelt is President of the United States. As part of his general reform program, The New Deal, he appoints John Collier as Commissioner of Indian Affairs. Collier introduces many reforms that Zitkala-Ša and Raymond had fought for, such as the Indian Reorganization Act, which ends the policy of allotment and encourages tribal governments.

March 13–15, 1935. A revised version of *The Sun Dance* is performed at Brigham Young University.

January 26, 1938. Zitkala-Ša dies.

April 27, 1938. New York City Light Opera Guild performs *The Sun Dance*.

GLOSSARY

The individual nations within the confederation of the Great Sioux Nation of the Plains Indians comprised three distinct divisions: the Santees, living in the woodlands and prairies of Minnesota, centering along the Minnesota River; the Yanktons, living in the prairies east of the Missouri River in North and South Dakota; and the Tetons, living on the high plains west of the Missouri River in North and South Dakota. The Santees and Yanktons called themselves "Dakota," while the Tetons called themselves "Lakota." Each of the three peoples spoke distinctive dialects, but could converse and understand one another; their differences in pronunciation might be compared to English as spoken by people from England and English as spoken by citizens of the United States.

Sometimes the Yanktons are called the "Nakota" because their dialect uses an "n" frequently where Santee uses "d" and Lakota uses "l." However, this usage is incorrect, because the people who call themselves Nakota are Assiniboines of Montana, a nation only distantly related to the Sioux and speaking a very different dialect. The words and pronunciations in this glossary are in the Dakota dialect as spoken by the Yanktons, Zitkala-Ša's people. Ironically, the only exception to this is "Zitkala-Ša." For some unexplained reason, in giving herself an Indian name, Zitkala-Ša chose a Lakota dialect.

In the pronunciations, syllables in caps are stressed and the raised "n" usually indicates that the preceding vowel sound is pronounced through the nose (nasalized). Note that "n" following a vowel is not pronounced as a separate sound. Sometimes it is a true "n," but only when it starts a syllable.

Caġu   (chah-ROO)—"Lung."

Han! han!   (HA^n! HA^n!)—"Yes! yes!"

Hejáta   (hay-ZHAH-tah)—"Forked horn."

Hin! hin!   (HEE^n! HEE^n!)—An expression of disapproval.

Ihánktunwan   (ee-HAHNK-too^n-wa^n)—"End Village," the Yankton Sioux.

Ikmú   (eek-MOO)—"Wild Cat."

Iktomi   (eek-TOE-mee)—"Spider; the Trickster."

Judéwin   (zhoo-DAY-wee^n)—Most likely the name "Judith" given by Christian missionaries and linked with the Yankton "win," indicating "woman."

Ohiya   (oh-HEE-yah)—"Winner."

Taté Iyóhiwin   (tah-DAY ee-YO-hee-wee^n)—"Every Wind."

Totówin   (toe-TOE-wee^n)—"Blue Woman."

Tiyóṡpaye   (tee-YO-shpah-yay)—A social unit, band; extended family.

Waṡíčun   (wah-SHE-djoo^n)—"White man."

Waṡíčun kin owéwakankan táwapi   (wah-SHE-djoo^n kee^n o-WAY-wah-kah^n-kah^n TAH-wah-pee)—"White men's lies."

Waȟčáziwin   (wah-DJAH-zee-wee^n)—"Yellow Flower Woman."

Wínyan   (WEE^n-ya^n)—"Woman."

Wóniya Kin Tínta Kin Píyawanikiye   (WOE-nee-yah kee^n TEEN-tah kee^n PEE-yah-wah-nee-key-yay)—"The Breath That Brings Life to the Prairie."

Wóunspe Tokáheya   (WOE-oo^n-spay toe-KAH-hay-yah)—"First Lessons."

Zitkala-Ša   (zit-KAH-lah-shah)—"Red Bird."

SOURCES

The following explains how I re-created Zitkala-Ša's life. I hope this information proves helpful to others who wish to further explore her world. The Bibliography provides the particulars on publishing data. Much of the research material that I accumulated during the writing of this book has been deposited at the Regional History Center, Uintah County Library, Vernal, Utah.

"The Yankton Reservation" grew out of *Remember Your Relatives*, Volumes I and II; reports by the superintendents of the Yankton Reservation, 1875–1880; interviews with Yankton elders who recounted their lives at the turn of the century for the Institute for American Studies at the University of South Dakota and talks with Leonard Bruguier. The accounts of Zitkala-Ša's early life on the reservation were edited from her memoir in the *Atlantic Monthly*. Hazel Ashes provided information and insight about Zitkala-Ša's siblings and family life. She told me that her father, David, had never been given an Indian name; in Zitkala-Ša's memoir she had given him the Indian name of Dawée. I changed this and used the name he used. I retold the Iktomi legend based on a typewritten draft found in the Gertrude and Raymond Bonnin Papers.

"Red Apple Country" came from her memoir. Details about school routines, runaways, and parental responses were found in *Josiah White's Institute*, and John W. and Ruth Ann Parker's notes also clarified the length of Zitkala-Ša's stay and the health record of other In-dian children at the Institute. The *Wabash Times* described the final graduation.

"Between Two Worlds" came from Zitkala-Ša's memoir. The *Indi-anapolis News* described the contest. Her speech, "Side by Side," and details of her return celebration were found in *The Earlhamite*. The incident involving the surveyors was based on material in *Lessons from Choteau Creek*. Hazel Ashes told me about her parents' life. Zitkala-Ša's life in Boston, her friendships, and how she came to write her memoir were found in letters in the Gertrude and Raymond Bonnin Papers, as was the background on Raymond's family. The letters be-tween Carlos and Zitkala-Ša were taken from The Papers of Carlos Montezuma. Unfortunately, the records of the New England Conser-vatory of Music in the late 1800s were destroyed in a fire. I was unable to track down the last names of her friends Gracie and Ethel.

"The Uintah Reservation" was reconstructed from superintendents' reports, Raymond and Zitkala-Ša's letters, and autobiographical data found in the Gertrude and Raymond Bonnin Papers. The material on William Hanson's relationship with Zitkala-Ša and the opera is de-tailed in his book *The Sun Dance Land* and a handwritten manuscript in the William Hanson Papers. The *Vernal Express*, *Salt Lake City Tribune*, *Deseret News*, and *Musical Courier* printed articles about re-hearsals and performances. Zitkala-Ša described her work on the Uin-tah Reservation in the *Quarterly Journal of the Society of American Indians*. Her October 4, 1913, letter about her marital difficulties was found in the records of the Board of Catholic Missions. The Monte-

zuma letters come from The Papers of Carlos Montezuma. "The Indian's Awakening" was printed in the *American Indian Magazine*.

"Washington, D.C." covers her work in the Society of American
Indians and the National Council of American Indians. Essential for
understanding the pan-Indian movement was *The Search for An American Indian Identity*. The peyote testimony was taken from *Hearings
Before the Senate Subcommittee of the Committee on Indian Affairs,
69th Congress, 2nd session, 1918*. William Willard's "The First
Amendment, Anglo-Conformity and American Indian Religious Freedom," in *Wicazo Sa Review*, meticulously re-created Zitkala-Ša's role
in the struggle about peyote. Essential for understanding the situation
in Oklahoma were *And Still the Waters Run* and *The Deaths of Sybil
Bolton*; the vignettes come from *Oklahoma's Poor Rich Indians*. Letters in the Raymond and Gertrude Bonnin Papers described the years
in the NCAI. The Iktomi story is from *Old Indian Legends*.

The chapter "Despair" was reconstructed from Zitkala-Ša's diary
entries during the years 1936–1937.

BIBLIOGRAPHY

Selected Titles

Hanson, William. *The Sun Dance Land*. Provo, UT: J. Grant Stevenson, 1967.

Hirschfelder, Arlene, and Beverly Singer. *Rising Voices*. New York: Scribner's, 1992.

Hoover, Herbert, with Leonard R. Bruguier. *The Yankton Sioux*. New York: Chelsea House, 1988.

Sansom-Flood, Renée. *Lessons from Choteau Creek*. Sioux Falls, SD: Center for Western Studies, 1986.

—— and Shirley Bernie. *Remember Your Relatives: Yankton Sioux Images, 1851 to 1904*, Vol. I. Marty, SD: Yankton Indian School, 1985.

——, Shirley Bernie, and Leonard R. Bruguier. *Remember Your Relatives: Yankton Sioux Images, 1865 to 1915*, Vol. II. Marty, SD: Yankton Sioux Elderly Advisory Board, 1989.

U.S. Senate, Subcommittee on Indian Affairs, 65th Congress, 2nd Session, 1918. Hearings. Washington, D.C.: U.S. Government Printing Office, 1918.

Willard, William. "The First Amendment, Anglo-Conformity and American Indian Religious Freedom." *Wicazo Sa Review*, Vol. VII, No. 1, Spring 1991.

Zitkala-Ša. *American Indian Stories*. Boston: Ginn, 1921.

——. "Impressions of an Indian Childhood." *Atlantic Monthly*, Vol. 85, January 1900.

———. "An Indian Teacher Among Indians." *Atlantic Monthly*, Vol. 85, March 1900.

———. "The Indian's Awakening." *American Indian Magazine*, January–March 1916.

———. *Old Indian Legends*. Boston: Ginn, 1901.

———. "The School Days of an Indian Girl." *Atlantic Monthly*, Vol. 85, February 1900.

———. "Side by Side." Richmond, IN: *The Earlhamite*, Vol. 2, March 16, 1896.

———. "The Trial Path." *Harper's Magazine*, Vol. 103, October 1901.

———. "Why I Am a Pagan." *Atlantic Monthly*, Vol. 90, December 1902.

ADVANCED READING

Brown, Dee. *Bury My Heart at Wounded Knee*. New York: Henry Holt, 1970.

Brown, Joseph Epes, editor. *The Sacred Pipe: Black Elk's Account of the Seven Rites of the Oglala Sioux*. Norman, OK: University of Oklahoma Press, 1953.

Debo, Angie. *And Still the Waters Run*. Princeton, NJ: Princeton University Press, 1950.

Deloria, Ella C. *Dakota Texts*. Edited by Agnes Picotte and Paul N. Pavich. Reprint. Vermillion, SD: State Publishing Company, 1983.

———. *Speaking of Indians*. Edited by Agnes Picotte and Paul N. Pavich. Reprint. Vermillion, SD: State Publishing Company, 1983.

Deloria, Vine, Jr. *Custer Died for Your Sins*. New York: Macmillan, 1969.

◆ ◆ Bibliography ◆ ◆

Fisher, Dexter. *The Transformation of Tradition: A Study of Zitkala-Ša and Mourning Dove, Two Transitional American Indian Writers*. Dissertation, New York University, 1969.

Hertzberg, Hazel W. *The Search for an American Indian Identity*. Syracuse, NY: Syracuse University Press, 1971.

Iverson, Peter. *Carlos Montezuma and the Changing World of American Indians*. Albuquerque, NM: University of New Mexico Press, 1982.

McAuliffe, Dennis, Jr. *The Deaths of Sybil Bolton*. New York: Times Books, 1994.

Montezuma, Carlos. The Papers of Carlos Montezuma. Edited by John W. Larner, Jr. Wilmington, DE: Scholarly Resources, 1983, 9 microfilm reels.

Neihardt, John G., as told through. *Black Elk Speaks*. Lincoln, NE: University of Nebraska Press, 1988.

Parker, John W., and Ruth Ann Parker. *Josiah White's Institute*. Wabash, IN: White's Institute, 1983.

Welch, Deborah Sue. *Zitkala-Ša: An American Indian Leader, 1876–1938*. Ann Arbor, MI: University Microfilms International, 1985.

Zitkala-Ša, Charles H. Fabens, and Matthew K. Sniffen. *Oklahoma's Poor Rich Indians: An Orgy of Graft and Exploitation of the Five Civilized Tribes—Legalized Robbery*. Philadelphia: Office of the Indian Rights Association, 1924.

PERIODICALS

American Indian Magazine, Deseret News, Indianapolis News, Musical Courier, Quarterly Journal of the Society of American Indians,

Salt Lake City Tribune, Vernal (Utah) *Express*, *Wabash Times*, *Washington Times*.

Additional Readings About the Sioux Nation

Anderson, Peter. *Charles Eastman*. Chicago: Children's Press, 1992.

Crow Dog, Mary, and Richard Erdoes. *Lakota Woman*. New York: Weidenfeld, 1990.

Deloria, Ella C. *Waterlily*. Lincoln, NE: University of Nebraska Press, 1988.

Eastman, Charles. *Indian Boyhood*. Reprint. New York: Dover, 1971.

————. *From Deep Woods to Civilization*. Boston: Little, Brown, 1916.

————. *Smoky Days Wigwam Evenings: Indian Stories Retold*. Boston: Little, Brown, 1911.

————. *Wigwam Evenings: Sioux Folk Tales Retold*. Boston: Little, Brown, 1909.

Sandoz, Mari. *These Were the Sioux*. Lincoln, NE: University of Nebraska Press, 1985.

Standing Bear, Luther. *My People, the Sioux*. Lincoln, NE: University of Nebraska Press, 1975.

Yellow Robe, Rosebud. *Tonweya and the Eagles*. New York: Dial, 1979.

INDEX

Page numbers in *italics* refer to photographs.